ONE KNIGHT STAND : BLAINE

KAYCE KYLE

CONTENTS

KAYCE KYLE

COPYRIGHT

Legal

One Knight Stand: Blaine Book One
Copyright 2018 Kayce Kyle
Edited by: Darlene Tallman
Cover by: Shelly Morgan
Format by : Liberty Parker
Copyright © 2018 by Kayce Kyle

Kayce Kyle
Copyright © 2018
All rights reserved by Author
Cover art by: Reggie Deanching photographer @RplusMphoto
Cover Model: Cody Smith

SYNOPSIS

BLAINE

As a bar owner in a small town, I meet a lot of women. I bed most of them. No expectations and no strings attached. Am I ashamed of that? Not even a little. I have my reasons. I consider my life perfect the way things are. Until one stormy night *she* came barreling through the doors. Our eyes met, and in that moment, I knew the universe was conspiring against me. I harbor a secret that could destroy anything more than a one-time thing between us. Maybe that's all this is meant to be, and if so, I can handle that. Or can I? Will my family secret have her running back to the life she initially fled?

TARA

Born with a silver spoon in my mouth? No, more like platinum, adorned with the finest quality diamonds from around the world. Yes, I was born into a wealthy, elite family. Most would say I have it all, but I have nothing. Material things? Sure. That seems to be enough for everyone in my social class, but not for me. I long for something more. Something real. Love. A love so deep that you can't put a monetary value on it unlike everything else in my life. I've been groomed from birth to live and maintain what's socially accepted in this world of top elitists. Of course, that was before I looked into a pair of baby-blues that immediately set my heart on fire. Will he still accept me once all my deep, dark, secrets are revealed? Or will he break my heart, too?

DISCLAIMER AND NOTES TO READERS

This book includes explicit sexual content, violence, explicit language, and possibly sensitive emotional situations. Therefore, I would like to take this time to warn you that if any of the above could ignite fear, offend you, or trigger a painful past memory for you, please send the book back immediately. Nobody should ever have to endure any abuse. Sexual, or otherwise.

If you, or anyone you know are in an abusive relationship, or have been abused, it's not ever too late to reach out and ask for help.

A few numbers for outreach include 1-800-799-7233 / 1-800-787-3224 (TTY)

This book is rated for mature audiences eighteen and above.

CHARACTER AND BOOK INFORMATION

This is book one in the Knight brothers' duet. All characters are fictional, as is the story. It is all based on a vision—my vision. If there are certain names in this book you find familiar or have heard before, it is all purely coincidental—stemming from my imagination alone.

I am a self-publishing Author and all I ask is that you keep an open mind and follow me along this journey. Thank you kindly for riding out this inevitable adventure with me.

Also, there are slang words in this story. Not too many, but this is the way my characters chose to speak to me. It is not a grammatical or editing error. If you see certain words such as "gonna" or "wanna", those are very well meant to be written in that manner. However, should there be any editing errors, they would be of my own doing. I have a fabulous editor that makes the possibility of any errors less likely. Having said that, I am only human, and mistakes do happen.

PROLOGUE

BLAINE

"Bro, seriously? You've gotta stop doing whatever this is with Gwen. She's getting too damn comfortable around here. Thought you were ending this thing with her two fucks ago? You got real feelings or what?" my brother Emmit asks with narrowed eyes laced with frustration as he leans against the frame of my door.

"She still here?" I throw a shirt over my head as I stand, pulling a pair of my washed-out jeans on.

"Made her leave a few minutes ago when I found her once again making herself too cozy here. She had a pot of coffee going and was gathering food from the fridge to make breakfast. Blaine." He snaps his fingers at me, trying to gain my attention. "Did you hear what I said?"

Flicking my eyes to him as I fasten my belt buckle, I say, "Yes, Emmit. Breakfast. The meal most prepared by a woman for *her* man. Or one she's trying to sink her claws into. I'll end it. I agree, she's getting the wrong idea. Should've done it long ago anyway."

He grunts before a small chuckle erupts from his throat. "Bro, she's already got the wrong idea. You broke the number one rule. You've allowed her to warm your bed on multiple occasions. You know how chicks think." I turn to face him and watch as he chews on a toothpick. "I can see this going full-on fatal attraction. She's hot, yeah, but don't tell me you can't see how jealous she acts in here when other women have your attention? Whatever, you do what you want, but she seems like unwanted drama we don't want or need around the bar."

"I got it, Emmit!" I snap at him. "Now, I've still gotta eat, shower and get ready for our shipment that will be here shortly."

"Ma stopped by with some breakfast sandwiches shortly after Gwen left. I told her you were still sleeping, and she didn't want me to wake you. Said to make sure you ate. She had a hair appointment in town, so she couldn't stay." He pulls the toothpick from his mouth. "You shower, and your sandwich will be downstairs waiting for you."

"You're not ma, you know? But you sure are bossy like you're her," I say, pushing my way past him as I make my way downstairs. I'll eat first while my food is still somewhat warm. Ain't nothing on this planet as good as our ma's cooking.

I can hear the bounce of his steps following behind me. "Well, I am the big brother, and it's my job to protect you," his voice booms behind me.

Once I've made my way to the kitchen area, I locate the sandwich ma left for me and unwrap it. "You're one year older than me, Emmit. It's not your job and hasn't been since we were kids. Your job is to bartend, play bouncer, and stay out of my business," I tell him, sinking my teeth into my food.

Folding his arms over his chest, he replies, "Two days, Blaine. That's all we have left before this place is packed with thirsty townspeople as they cheer on the high school championship game. We're the only bar in this town and shit's gonna get real. You know how serious everyone takes this. And since they've made it to state, we need to be prepared. This hasn't happened in over thirty years. It's me, you, and Sharla running this place. We need more hands on deck."

With a mouthful of food, I try not to choke on my laughter at the seriousness and anxiety in his tone. "How serious *everyone* takes this, Emmit?" I lower my gaze to the worn out t-shirt his folded arms partially cover. "Are you lumping yourself into that category?" Emmit was a jock in high school. He was our varsity quarterback, and still bitter to this day they lost their first playoff game. His eyes turn to slits and I watch him fight the urge to defend himself. "We've got this. I don't want to hire anyone else. You know this. We've been over it a thousand times. What makes us unique is that we're family-owned. People know and trust us. We're a small town and I don't ever wanna change the vibe of this place because we've got some money now. We're a town of generational farmers and lower to middle class people. We said this money from the woman who birthed us wouldn't change us. Let's keep that promise, huh?"

"Fuck, Blaine. You act like I was suggesting we hire an entire staff serving from gold-plated platters and bottles of high-end champagne with flecks of gold inside. I'm just saying that I think we are short-staffed for this night...*and* that you're still clouded with pussy brain," he spouts off.

"I'm not budging," I rebuttal, passing back by him. "I'm headed upstairs to shower." I take another bite of my breakfast. "Hopefully the soap will sink into my scalp and into my brain. You know, washing away any residual pussy brain as you just called it. Try getting some every now and then. Maybe you'll be less uptight. Damn. You used to fuck anything with a pussy between their legs. Lighten up."

"Fuck you, little brother," he shouts behind me, as I continue back up the stairs to my room with a smirk on my face he can't see.

CHAPTER ONE

TARA

"Reservations at the Skyfall. He bought you a dress and had it delivered to you from Nordstrom's along with a pair of new Jimmy Choo's," my sister Rachel gushes, as she all but fondles and caresses the heels against her cheek. "Who knows what else he has planned, Tara." She wiggles her brows at me. "This is it, he's going to ask you to marry him and you'll finally become Mrs. Preston Hallister. You'll be the envy of every woman in town."

I wish I could say that she's wrong, but I feel like she's right, and that's the problem. "Yes, Mrs. Preston Hallister," I say out loud. My words come out strained, voicing my concern.

"Don't get too excited, Tara. You wouldn't want to let your enthusiasm cause a mild panic attack or anything," she sarcastically states, placing the designer heels back in the box. "Mom's already started calling wedding planners you know?"

Ah, yes, my mother. Of course, she has. The biggest hypocrite to ever walk among the great elites of Dallas, Texas. Rachel and I are the only children of my parents, Edward and Katherine Billings. My father is a real estate mogul who rubs elbows with politicians, professional athletes, and celebrities. My mother married into my father's money. Rachel and I have never wanted for a single thing in life, well, not anything that money could buy. My sister is the perfect protégé. She's as brainwashed, money and power hungry as they've trained her to be. I was too, once. Although I always wanted something more and knew something was missing from my life.

Foolishly, I'd let myself believe that Preston was everything I wanted and was willing to provide more than just a lifestyle. I already have my own money and more than I can probably spend in a lifetime, I don't need more. What I crave is real love and genuine affection. Again, I thought I had that with Preston…at first. That was until a few weeks ago. He was working late at his father's office and what will be his one day, so I decided to surprise him with a romantic dinner. I'd ordered from our favorite upscale

Italian restaurant and picked it up. I'd even grabbed some candles hoping to make it somewhat romantic considering he'd been putting in so many hours at the office. I knew he was out to prove to his father that he was ready to take over Hallister Enterprises, so I hadn't put up any arguments. I put on his favorite little red dress of mine and primped myself to perfection. Only when I arrived, I found him at his desk with his secretary bent over it while he fucked her like he'd never fucked *me* before.

I left. He never knew I was there. Feelings of devastation, loss, fury, heartbreak, and defeat have now become some of my truest friends. I haven't had the courage to tell anyone, except Carmen. She was mine and Rachel's nanny until we became adults. She has always been more of a mother to us than our own. Now, since we're both adults, she's my family's trusted housekeeper. So, yes, I dread Preston asking me to marry him, because I'm not sure that I can. It might sound silly to most. It should be cut and dry. Black and white, right? I wish it were, but someone with my social standing doesn't have many options. Everyone knows everyone, and the women don't usually dare say no or cross their men. Yes, we live in modern times, but in our society specifically, the men have the power to destroy a woman and any future romantic partner. Even though Preston is the one who is a lying, filthy, cheater, so are most of the other men. Again, they have the power and know it. I remember when I was around sixteen years old hearing my parents arguing. I was eavesdropping, and my mother was shouting through her sobs as she blasted my father for cheating *again*. It was like a knife to my heart and I couldn't imagine how my mother felt. My father told her words that I remember to this day. He said, "Katherine, you came from nothing, and that's exactly what you'll be if you try to go public and divorce me. I'll ruin you. Don't forget about the prenuptial agreement."

"Earth to Tara." My sister waves her hands in front of my face. "What are you so deep in thought about? Is it Preston? What if he takes one of his father's jets and takes you to Paris? Or what if…" she continues, but I stand up and shake my head as I place my hand up, silently ordering her to stop.

My palms are sweaty and I'm not even sure if he's going to propose. All of this could be for nothing. One thing is for sure, though, I've got to figure out how to end things with Preston without compromising my reputation. I do have my own money and my own penthouse apartment. "Rach, calm down, would you? Why don't you let me take this one day, and one step at a time?"

"Fine," she mutters. "I can't stand it anymore!" She jumps up and grabs me by the shoulders. "He asked Daddy's permission two weeks ago! It's true! I heard him and Mom talking about it a few nights ago! He's going to do it on your birthday at the party planned for you. Which you're also not supposed to know about. Now, will you go ahead and start getting excited?"

My heart pounds relentlessly inside my chest at her declaration. She's always been nosy and terrible at keeping secrets. Shit, until she mentioned it, I'd forgotten about my birthday. The last year I'll spend in my twenties. Waves of panic crash and wash over me, leaving me drenched as I drown in apprehension. This can't happen. Telling him no will humiliate him, especially in a room full of powerful elitists. "M-my birthday?" My words come out shaky as I wring my hands together.

My sister shakes her head. "Yes, they've got an announcement written and ready to go out in the newspaper the morning after. Isn't it like a dream come true?" she muses, her eyes glossed over and shiny like the diamond she viciously craves to be placed on her own finger. I love my sister, but she's a product of her environment. She's still a year away from receiving her trust fund inheritance, and she's still blissfully ignorant at only twenty years old. She hasn't seen or heard the things that I have. Maybe I should've shared those things with her, but given our parents were barely a part of our lives, I never wanted to taint any memories or preconceived ideas she has about them.

"A nightmare," I mumble, shifting my gaze toward the floor not meaning for that to slip out verbally.

"A what?" she snaps. "Did you just call getting engaged to *the* most eligible bachelor in Dallas a nightmare?"

"No." I lie to her face. "I said I feel light as air. Now, I have a shopping date with Cynthia. I need to change and get ready. Oh, and Rachel? Please, please don't tell anyone you told me. You'll just ruin the surprise and Preston will be angry with you. He might tell Cameron and then you could lose your chance at ever having any real shot with him." Cameron is another member of our high-society's up and coming and Rachel's age. She's been drooling over him for months now. So, using this to subtly threaten her is my best shot at having her keep her lips sealed. "Now, I'll call you tomorrow and maybe we can set up a spa day? You know, so I can be as relaxed and beautiful as possible before the big day." Her eyes grow wide along with the grin on her face as she hugs me, and I feel guilt ridden for lying to her. I should've ended things with Preston weeks ago, but he's never here, and when he is I seem to lose all my courage. I usher her out of my apartment. Once she's gone, frantically, I text Carmen and ask her to meet me at the coffee shop down the street from my place after she leaves work.

BLAINE

THE SUN BEGINS TO SET AND IT'S TIME TO OPEN THE DOORS again for another night of booze, music, billiards, and bar fights. Before I head over to open the doors for business, Sharla uses her key and bursts through one of the front doors. She races past me and behind the bar where she stows away her purse and pours herself a quick shot of whiskey. "You're late again, Sharla."

"And you're still an ass, Blaine," she retorts, slamming down the gold liquid as she shudders at its potency. I hear Emmit chuckle from behind the bar where he's polishing beer mugs. "You know these classes I'm taking are during the day, right? When you two boneheads are recovering and getting the sleep you need, I'm studying. Plus, Raymond stopped by today wanting to see Jett and, well, we got into it. So, please, spare me the lecture and cut me a break. You know I'm busting my ass here."

I glance at Emmit as the blood in my veins begins to boil. Emmit is only one wrong word away from beating Raymond to a bloody pulp. Raymond is a piece of shit loser and waste of space even in our small town, but he's Jett's father. Jett's their four-year-old son. We've known Sharla since we were about ten years old and her family moved in next door to ours. She's like a sister to us and even more so after her parents were killed in a car accident when she was pregnant with Jett. She and Ray were high school sweethearts. She's always been too good for him, and he's always been a loser. Our ma watches Jett while Sharla works, and her neighbor helps with him sometimes while she studies. She can most certainly be feisty, but she's always been a caring person and a natural caregiver. So, when she decided to go back to get a degree to work in the medical field as a CNA, none of us were surprised.

Walking up to the bar, I rest my elbows on the wooden counter. "Did he lay a hand on you?" I reach across and grab for her wrists, but she yanks them away.

"No. And he hasn't since the night the both of you threw him out of here for good. I guess you both scared him good." She shrugs, almost offended that I would ask.

Emmit sighs heavily. "The fucker better stay away from you if he likes his head attached to his shoulders."

Sharla giggles as she takes money from the safe and fills the register drawer. "That would insinuate he has a brain in that head of his, and I'm pretty sure it relocated to his dick years ago." She slams the register drawer shut. "Anyway, he may have treated me shitty, but he's Jett's father. It's not Jett's fault his dad's a piece of shit."

I walk over to the old jukebox we have in here to keep the

feel of the bar country and cozy and turn her on. As I walk back behind the bar, I pat Sharla on the back. "Sorry about snapping at ya. I know you've got a lot on your plate and I wouldn't dream of adding more, you know that. Between Emmit stressing me out about the big game tomorrow night and trying to get everything ready, I'm on edge."

"Oh, you don't need *me* for you to be a fucking dick. You manage to do that extremely well on your own." Emmit glares at me and I offer up my middle finger in exaggerated appreciation.

The doors begin to open, and people pile in one after another.

TARA

"Sweetie, your text sounded urgent. Are you okay?" I jump, startled as Carmen's hand briefly makes contact with my back before she sits across from me at the round glass table I've reserved for us.

Removing my sunglasses that have been hiding my tear-stained cheeks and swollen eyes, I hardly take a breath between words, "Preston's going to ask me to marry him in less than forty-eight hours. Which I'm sure you already know about and, well, as you know, the bastard cheated on me. I've been on autopilot these past few weeks and haven't confronted him. Hell, I've barely seen him. So, having to have sex with him after the fact hasn't been a topic. I'm sure he's screwing some whore at work anyway."

Taking my hands into hers from across the table, she squeezes them. "Tara, my sweet girl. Slow down. Breathe."

I pull one of my hands from hers and begin to fan myself as I blow out deep heavy breaths. "I can't, Carmen. You know I can't. I won't." I shake my head looking down, attempting to ward off any more of the tears awaiting their chance to burst free.

"First of all, look at me," Carmen demands, and I slowly turn my eyes up and back to hers. "I did not know about this. I have heard and seen a lot within those walls over the years, but this I have not heard of. Not until now. Your mother has been happier than usual. She's been making and taking more private calls the past few days, but nothing to alert me that this was going on. What makes you think this?"

"Rachel. She told me she'd overheard my parents discussing it and that Preston had already asked my fathers permission. He's got this elaborate plan apparently for my birthday party." I swipe the tears away that have found freedom and slid down my cheeks.

Carmen releases my hand and sits back in her chair before she folds her arms over her chest and shakes her head. "Rachel, God love her, but she couldn't keep a secret if her life depended on it. She's a big mouth, yes, but she's not a liar. You have to confront him, Tara. Do it at your parents' house tomorrow. He wouldn't dare cause a scene in front of them. Your parents on the other hand, now they might be the ones to cause a scene. That bastard. Hurting my Tara this way." She leans forward, extending her open palms inviting my hands into hers. "I knew he was bad news from the start. I will be there too, for moral support."

"I don't know if I can. Even if I can, you're right, my parents will freak out if I dump him. You and I both know they'd play their part in the moment as I confront him about cheating. But as soon as he left, they'd be trying to convince me to give him a second chance. That everybody makes mistakes." I swallow the large lump that's formed in my throat before I take a sip of my sparkling water.

"Call him. Call him now. Set it up," she orders me. Pulling her hands from mine, she starts gesturing toward my handbag where my cell currently resides. Gosh, she's such a strong woman and she raised me more than my own mother did. Why do I feel so weak and hesitant about this when I know there's no way in hell I'll ever marry the lying piece of shit? Not now. Reaching inside my purse, I retrieve my cell. Looking at Carmen once more, she nods her head in encouragement, giving me the strength I need to place this call. Holding the phone to my ear, I whisper across the table, "It's ringing." The loud rhythmic thud of my own heartbeat pounds in my ears as ring after ring, he never picks up. Eventually, I get his voicemail. Of course. "Voicemail," I whisper to her, and she nods her head again and flicks her wrist, silently encouraging me to leave him a message. My nerves sneak up and grab me, taking me hostage and I quickly end the call without leaving a voicemail before placing my phone down on the table.

"Tara Elizabeth Billings, I am disappointed. Why, sweetie, why?" she pleads for an answer from me, taking my hands into hers once again.

"I-I just can't, Carmen. I can't talk to him. He'll sense something's off in my tone. Of course, he'd have to answer first." I feel my eyes shift as they roll in agitation. "Please don't be disappointed in me." I squeeze her hands. "I'll figure it out, and by tomorrow. I promise." I stand from my chair and she does the same. I pull her into my arms as the wheels in my head begin to spin. I know what I'm going to do. I'll just come up with an excuse after the fact. I can't tell her because the less she knows, the better.

At least she can look and act as shocked as the rest of them without having to lie to their faces.

After our embrace, she kisses my cheek. "Don't do anything irrational, Tara. You're emotional right now. When we act on pure emotion, the repercussions can be catastrophic. Like a baby bird learning to fly, we're either going to find ourselves planted face first on the concrete. Or, we luck out and fly. The latter of the two is a rarity." She cups the side of my cheek and I lean into her motherly comfort. "Remember that *always* my sweet girl. If you need me, call me."

I nod as my heart shatters inside knowing it's time to part ways for now. She hesitates, but eventually turns and walks away. I want to curl up in her lap as I did as a little girl when I was upset. She'd run her fingers through my hair as she held me close and sang to me. It was so comforting and most of my friends all felt the same way about their nanny's, too. Not a single one of us could share a story of either of our parents ever treating us this way or tending to our broken little hearts.

After returning to my penthouse, I receive a text from Preston apologizing for missing my call. He proceeds to tell me he's working late and not to wait up for him tonight. Shocker. His lies and dirty little secrets make *me* feel filthy. I shower hoping to wash away some of that feeling before changing into some comfortable yoga pants and a tank top. After what feels like hours of flipping through the channels on my television, nothing has managed to find and hold my attention. Now, all I can seem to do is pace the floor to my apartment.

———

THE STARTLING RING FROM MY PHONE WAKES ME. RUBBING my eyes, I reach over and glance at the screen to see that my sister's calling. Shit. I told her yesterday that we'd have a spa day today. Ignoring her call, I Spring from my bed. Racing to the bathroom, I brush my teeth, hair, and change into a pair of jeans and casual off-the-shoulder top. I finish my ensemble off with a pair of wedges before I gloss my lips and place my sunglasses on. Hastily, I grab my purse as I head toward the elevator door of my penthouse floor apartment.

Placing my hand on my chest briefly as I inhale deeply, I feel the single two-carat diamond stud Preston had made into a necklace around my neck. It stops me in my tracks and everything leading up to this moment comes crashing down at once, nearly dropping me to the floor. My heart thunders inside my chest as it beats erratically, and I can no longer take it. I've got to get out of here; even if only for a few days. At least until after my birthday. Looking down to grab my keys off the sofa table a picture of Preston and I catches my attention. We look so happy. So content. What a fool I was to let myself believe that I had found the perfect man, that he was different than the rest. I feel for the necklace that still hangs like a prize from my neck and yank it off. I place it in front of the framed picture before I turn it face down and leave my penthouse. I have zero clue where I'm going, but right now, I don't care. My instinct is to run, and that's just what I'm going to do.

CHAPTER TWO

BLAINE

Tonight's the big night, and as much shit as I've given Emmit, tonight is huge for this town and this bar. Rose City, Texas doesn't have much going for it, but we're all family in a sense. In such a small town like ours, everyone knows everyone. High School football, tailgating, and bonfires are what we do. It's our life and what we know. Are we considered hillbilly's or rednecks by some? You're damn right. Do we give a fuck? Hell no. Some people are either born into and are suited for that fast-paced city life. Hell, I pity those fuckers. No wonder they're all so uptight. I couldn't imagine having to wake up each morning and sliding myself into some fancy tailored nut-hugging suit with my feet all cramped up into some

Italian leather name brand shoes. Nah, this right here is the life. Slow-paced, comfortable, and not a single person to answer to or yapping in my ear. Well, besides Emmit and our ma occasionally. Those are the only two I will probably ever be able to stand in my ear. I've done the whole relationship thing when I was in my early twenties. Natalie the lying, cheating, slut. Yep, that's what I call her. Bitch temporarily stole my heart and when she found her a man passing through town that had a little bit of money, she shagged ass and left me in the dust. Those rich fuckers are all the same. Look down on people such as myself, but my goddamn alcohol and establishment is good enough for them when they want something. Typical hypocrisy from someone born with a platinum spoon in their mouth. I refuse to allow another woman to ever have that sort of control over me. Relationships aren't for me, and I refuse to budge.

Aside from our parent's and Sharla, nobody knows Emmit and I are loaded after our birth mother passed and left us millions a piece. It's nobody's business and I plan on keeping it that way. It helps separate the loyal people from the money hungry gold-diggers. Emmit and I never have to wonder or question anyone's motives toward us. Yes, there are some women still looking for their ticket out of here. And finding it on their backs seems to be the way they go about it. My money sits untouched and in a savings account accruing interest. I like to pretend that shit doesn't exist, although consciously I know it does.

"Psycho alert!" I hear Sharla holler out from downstairs. "Your favorite, or shall I say, most recent bed buddy is banging on the front door of the bar calling out your name. Want me to let her in? Kick her ass? I can do both if you prefer."

I scrub my face with my palm and let out a heavy sigh. I told her last night I was completely done with her. "Nope! I'll handle her," I yell out, as I begin to make my way downstairs, taking them two at a time.

Ugh, Gwen's pounding on the bar doors and voice are the equivalent to nails on a fucking chalkboard. I unlock the door, but before I can open it fully, she shoves it, pushing me backward. "Karen? Really, Blaine? You sticking your cock in that slut again?" She shoves her finger into my chest in between each word.

What's this bitch talking about? I haven't fucked Karen in, hell I can't even remember. Arching a single brow, I cross my arms over my bare chest. "I owe you nothing, Gwen. And where I put my cock is none of your business. Never was. Now, get the fuck out before I call Sheriff Hall."

I feel someone approach me from behind and glance over my shoulder to see Sharla glaring at Gwen. "This is rich coming from a woman I once caught fucking my man when I was eight months pregnant. In my bed no less." Sharla tries to step around me, and I hold my arm up to stop her and Emmit is in front of her but behind me in seconds as if he's protectively guarding her. "Get the fuck out of here before the only people being called are the fucking county medical examiner's office when I'm finished with you!"

Gwen's mouth parts and a look of shock etches across her face. "This isn't over! You're all a bunch of fucking losers who will never have anything more than this bar! And that will never change!" I grab her arm and usher her back toward the door.

"You're a pathetic slut that will spread her legs for any man in this town. And *that* will never change." Sharla finishes taunting her before I shove Gwen out the door and lock it back behind me.

Running my hand through the top of my hair, I ask Sharla, "That true? Did Ray really fuck her when you were pregnant with Jett? Why didn't you ever tell us?"

She blows out a heavy sigh and turns on her heel. "Does it really matter now, Blaine?"

Shame and remorse wash over me for ever having that bitch in my bed or allowing her to step foot in this bar. "Yeah, it does fucking matter. I would've never allowed that bitch in here. Or in my bed. Just like Ray is banned, so is Gwen. Emmit, put her on the list." Making my way to the back to check our stock and make sure we've triple checked everything, I mumble, "No idea where that Karen nonsense came from. She sat here at the bar last night for hours hitting on me, but I saw right through her desperation."

"That would be Emmit," Sharla answers, never missing a beat as she checks off the list on her clipboard.

I stop and look back to see my brother just in time for him to swallow so hard it's audible. "What?" He tosses his hands in the air. "She was rubbing all up on my jock last night and I had one too many drinks." He raises a finger and points to me. "Don't you dare say a word. You know as well as I do that even Karen looks appealing with those beer goggles on."

I smirk in retaliation to the truth of his words. "Unfortu-nately, yes, I do. Wait. Sharla how did you know?" I shift my gaze to her, but she never looks up at me as she gnaws on the end of her pen cap. "She was leaving this morning as I was coming in. I wasn't sure which one of you she'd bedded, but now I know." If I didn't know better, I'd say I sense a hint of jealousy in her voice. I look over at Emmit who simply turns and walks away.

"Stop!" I order him and catch Sharla's full attention as her eyes meet mine. "Tonight's the night we've been waiting on. We've busted our asses extra fucking hard to make tonight perfect. Let's not get sidetracked now all because Gwen showed up and made a fool of herself. Let's get refocused and make tonight epic." I close my eyes for a fleeting moment and inhale deeply. "Something tells me tonight is gonna be a night we'll never forget. This will go down in 'One Knight Stands' history books!"

My pep talk does very little and they both grumble before getting back to work.

TARA

I'VE DRIVEN FOR HOURS UPON HOURS NOW. I'VE BLASTED my radio and sang the breath right out of my lungs all while managing to cry, too. The sun has long left and went to bed, while the moon is now awake and helping light my way through this darkness. Glancing down at my clock I realize it's past ten o'clock. I have no clue where I'm at exactly. Pulling my car over onto the shoulder of the free-way, I type in the nearest five star hotel. Unlucky for me, the closest one is over an hour back in the opposite direc-tion. I glance over at my cell resting in the soft leather passenger seat and pick it up. Sixteen missed calls and twelve text messages. I despise what my family stands for and allows on the best of days, but it would still be cruel to let them assume the worst. Surprisingly, several of those calls and texts were from the lying cheater himself. Quickly, I send both Carmen and my sister a text message letting them both know that I'm okay. Only there's one subtle difference in the one I send Carmen. I told her that no matter what, I was determined to be the rarity she spoke of no matter the cost. I asked her to trust me and assured her that I would be back soon enough and not to worry.

After I've turned my car completely around, my navigation takes me down a desolate, two-lane highway of some sort. Surrounded by complete darkness, tiny rain pellets begin to fall and gloss over my windshield. My nerves begin to take hold and my grip around the steering wheel stiffens and I can feel my skin tighten as my knuckles turn white. "You people don't believe in street lights or what?" I ask aloud, from the shelter of my car as I slow my speed.

This road is creepy and gives me an eerie feeling. Now all I want to do is go home and wrap myself up in one of my faux fur blankets and curl up next to my fireplace. Maybe finally open that bottle of two-thousand-five Chateau Petrus I was saving for a special occasion.

The rain picks up as the drops begin to pound loudly on the roof of my Lexus LC. Silently I begin to sob inside as I regret my decision to leave my apartment. Glancing down briefly at my navigation to see how much longer I have until I will arrive at my destination, the loud pop of my tire can be felt and heard as I desperately attempt to maintain control. I need to stop. I have to pull over. I'm going to be stuck on the isolated road of death until whatever lurks in those woods eventually finds me and comes out to feed on me. Turning on my hazard lights, I come to a complete stop. I'm emotionally and mentally exhausted and about to burst from every seam in my body. My face falls into my palms and I begin to wail before self-pity turns to pure unfiltered anger. Unable to control what's left of my emotions, my hands connect with the steering wheel as I pound my anger out on it.

BLAINE

"THEY WON! THEY FUCKING PULLED IT OFF WITH THAT two-point conversion and three seconds left on the clock!" Emmit squeezes the top of my shoulders in excitement before he pops off the cap on a beer and chugs it down.

Cheers have been ongoing now for well over a full minute. "One round of drinks on the house for the win! Go Dawgs!" I declare over the crowd, and another loud ring of excitement pierces my ears.

Sharla passes behind me and pats my back. "Good game, and great night, boss! Everyone's so pumped they're being extra generous with their tips. Looks like I'll be able to catch the rest of my bills up all by myself." She winks at me. "I do appreciate you and Emmit always looking out for me, though."

"Always," I reply as she walks back behind me the other way with a tray full of prepared drinks.

"Hey," I call out, and she stops and turns to look at me over her shoulder. "Gonna take this trash out to the dumpster. It's overflowing. I'll be right back."

"Got your colt?" she asks me, raising a single brow.

I reach behind myself and pat the lower part of my back where I keep my handgun on me at all times.

"Just be careful. That bobcat's still hunting close by and on the loose. Read it in the paper this morning. Got old man Stan's new calf," she informs me.

"I'm good," I tell her as I gather the overflowing trash bag and walk toward the back and outside the doors. The heavy rain pellets soak me in mere seconds, so I rush to the side where our main dumpster is and toss the bag over.

As I begin to turn my back to jog my way back inside, I hear the cry of a woman's voice call out, "Help! Can you help me, please?" It stops me where I stand, and I turn.

Through my blurred watery vision I attempt to make out where the voice is coming from. It gets closer and underneath the one street light hovering over the bar's parking lot, I see the small frame of a woman. She simply stands there as the rain beats down on her and I'm unsure if this is some escapee from an institution or what. Placing my hand around my backside and on my gun, slowly I approach her.

"Lady are you injured?" I holler out as I continue making my way closer. Still, she doesn't move which is suspicious, but she finally speaks.

"My car. I have a flat. A little way down there." She looks over her shoulder and points back down the road before turning her attention back to me.

"Okay. Let's get you inside and out of this weather and we can see about getting someone to help you." I'm now within a foot of her and I notice that she's definitely not anyone I recognize and must not be from around here. She's shivering, and fear plasters her face. "Look, I can see that you're not from around here. It's fucking raining, we're both drenched, and, well, there's a bobcat out here somewhere on the prowl. Not sure about you, but I'd rather not be its meal for the night."

Her trembling momentarily subsides as I watch her eyes grow large and she walks past me hastily, eventually turning into a jog to the front door of the bar. I'm right on her heels and make it past her in time to open the door for her and she quickly enters.

All eyes turn, and the entire bar seems to go silent. Most patrons in here are men tonight and they're all fairly buzzed if not flat-out drunk. Whistles and sexual advances are loudly voiced, but before I can say anything, she quickly turns and nearly walks right into me. My hands immediately find their way to the top of her shoulders as I try to assure her she's safe. I can clearly tell she's distraught and something tells me it's not simply over a flat tire.

Slowly, she brings her eyes up to meet mine. Mascara drips down her cheeks, but nothing takes away the absolute beauty of her bright golden-colored eyes peeking up at me through her lashes. So pure looking. I find myself their hostage as I want to dive into their innocence and wash away all the sins of my past. She swallows hard which only accentuates her neckline as she does so, and my eyes trail lower to her soaking wet shirt. Oh, shit! It's white, drooping off one shoulder, and the outline of her perky breasts and erect nipples are on full display. My cock twitches in my jeans. Even though my own shirt is soaking wet, I quickly remove it and wrap it around her as best I can. I can feel the heat of her gaze still fixated on me, but right now I cannot get lost in that again. "I'm Blaine." I gently place a hand on her arm and she jumps slightly.

"This is my bar. You're safe. I won't let those men harm you." Fuck, I don't know if she's been through some sort of domestic situation or what and I'm completely out of my element now. "You said you had a flat?" She nods.

"What's going on, Blaine?" Sharla approaches and asks, looking at me and then to the beauty that seemingly appeared out of nowhere. "Oh, honey. What's happened?" Sharla asks, with concern as she places her hand on this woman's arm.

"I'm gonna call Sheriff Hall," I say, as I start to walk past them both.

A hand grabs my arm, causing me to stop and turn back around. It's her, and those eyes dare me to try and look away, and I can't. "I'm Tara. I-I…am not hurt. Not physically. I have a flat tire not too far down the road out there. I'm just kind of far from home." Entranced by her angelic voice and held captive yet again by her eyes, I find myself rendered speechless. Tara, huh? Such an elegant name and she wears it beautifully and speaks it with such pride. Drenched from the rain this woman is still the most beautiful creature I've ever laid eyes on. She lowers her head, freeing me from their prison and I feel myself sigh. What in the fuck is happening here? "I just need a place to dry off and call someone to remove my car from that road, so it doesn't cause an accident."

"You go call the sheriff and I'm gonna take her upstairs and get her a dry t-shirt if that's okay?" Sharla asks me.

I run my hand through my hair as I once again find my eyes trailing back downward in hopes of stealing another view of her perfect tits.

"Blaine!" Sharla's voice startles me and my eyes snap up and find hers.

"What? Oh. Right. Yeah. That's fine," I finally answer, before turning on my heel as I make my way back behind the bar to call Sheriff Hall.

CHAPTER THREE

TARA

I MUST BE HAVING A DREAM WITHIN A NIGHTMARE. THIS place smells of thick cigarette smoke and cheap alcohol. My emotions border between feeling like I've entered an alternate universe while the other part of me is wildly curious. My eyes inquisitively follow Blaine as he walks over and behind the bar. My mouth waters at the very sight of this man and his perfectly built physique. His touch on my arm sent a jolt of electricity through my body as if it were breathing life back into it. A simple, harmless touch from him did more to my body than years of sex with Preston.

He oozes sex appeal and danger. His top left shoulder and chest is inked, something you don't typically see from men within our social standing. The way he instinctively covered me with his own shirt like a gentleman also intrigues me. There are a few women in here, but the limited amount of them that I see are following him with their eyes. He's the epitome of everything my family and friends would call trash and judge instantly, but the few simple acts he's done for me already have awakened sleeping butterflies in my stomach.

I've never actually been inside any place like this. There's a billiards table that looks as old as I am, and a torn leather sofa in the corner by it. A rather small bar counter top and on the other side of the bar, there's an old jukebox and I suppose the world's tiniest dance floor considering there were a few people dancing on it.

The woman who stepped in to help me hooks her arm through mine, as she begins to lead me somewhere. After we pass the jukebox and dance floor, the woman helping me ushers me to some stairs. I stop and turn to look at her skeptically. "Tara is it?" I nod after a brief moment. "I'm Sharla. Look, I know none of these buffoons know or have noticed, but I see that designer handbag locked onto your other elbow. You might not be in your fanciest clothes, but you're…well-kept." She eyes me up and down. "Not sure what brought you out this way, but right now, let's at least get you into a dry shirt. I know this is probably a place you wouldn't frequent if given a choice, but you kinda don't have one right now. Well, at least not until you buy your way out of this situation." I think she's just insulted me, but she's right. I'll be out of here rather soon. "So, all I'm asking is for a little bit of trust. We don't typically get women of your kind. Look, you're stunning and even with mascara-stained cheeks, you look like a barbie doll. So, it kinda made all these drunk bastards froth at the mouth. That's why Blaine tried to cover you with his shirt. He's harmless. Promise."

"Okay," I answer, as I clutch my purse closer to me and begin my journey up the stairs with Sharla's hand gently placed on the middle of my back behind me.

What am I thinking? Why am I so easily trusting this woman, and that man named Blaine? I might be a wealthy trust fund snob to some, but that doesn't mean I never went to a movie theater. Hell, I've seen those movies where someone ends up in a scenario similar to this only to wind up into tiny fragments left to rot in a field somewhere. Yet somehow, instinctively I trust them.

The stairs lead directly to a door and Sharla pulls a key from her apron and opens it. "Go on. Go in," she says, gesturing for me to proceed with her hand.

I enter the room and notice the room is bare bones only equipped with a bed, chair in the corner, a tiny dresser, and a nightstand with a lamp on it. Is this where Blaine sleeps? I nearly shudder at the thought. I would feel claustrophobic living like this day in and day out. Although I must admit, it's rather tidy. I wonder if he has a girlfriend who cleans up after him?

"Here, throw this on." Sharla's voice pulls me from scanning and scrutinizing his room. It's a pair of men's sweatpants and a t-shirt that will swallow me whole. "Or, you can stay in the soaking wet clothes you have on. I'd at least cover up your ta-ta's if you stay in those. Those puppies are perky and not leaving a damn thing to the imagination if you catch my drift?" She lowers her gaze to my chest.

I set my handbag down on the bed. Does she expect me to strip down and change right here in front of her? I briefly scan the room again to make sure I didn't miss a closet or restroom. I really do need out of these wet clothes. "Could you…" I begin, but she cuts me off.

"Turn around?"

I nod but take notice of her subtle eye roll as she turns away from me. I am wearing a bra, but Sharla's right—it's drenched, and you can see everything. At least the t-shirt she gave me is black. Once I have removed my clothing and have the new, dry shirt on, I bend over to pull the sweatpants up.

"Whoa!" I hear the deep rumble of a man's voice echo behind me, causing me to jump as I hastily finish pulling the sweatpants up. "Nice ass!"

"Pig!" Sharla shouts and it sounds like she smacks him in some manner.

"Give the lady some privacy, Emmit!" I hear Blaine's voice roar right after, as I turn around. I can feel the warmth creep up my neck and cheeks subtly burn them as I know the hint of my embarrassment shades my face. "Due to the weather, we're gonna be closing early. Sheriff Hall says the roads are beginning to flood."

Wait. Flood? Oh, no! This can't be happening. Not tonight and not to me. I have to get my tire fixed and at the very least get out of here. Damn, why does Blaine's voice stir up excitement inside of me that's apparently been dormant? Briefly I imagine how it might not be so bad being stuck here with him, at least for one night. It would definitely be something I've never experienced. Mentally, I rid myself of my last thoughts as I faintly shake it off.

"I've already started closing out tabs. Big Boy should have your car towed into this parking lot around back with our vehicles soon," Blaine looks at me and says, placing a hand on the doorframe. "You two should probably get back down there. It's gonna be a long night of cleaning up, too. I'll be right behind y'all," he states to Sharla and the man he called Emmit. The gentle stir of those butterflies begin to make their presence known again. Blaine's excusing them, and it will be just the two of us. In here, and alone. With a bed. Internally, I shame myself for allowing my mind to even think such things. But I'd be a liar if I didn't admit images of him touching and worshipping my bare skin while inside of me didn't just cross it.

"Damn, and I was hoping to break an even grand tonight. Eh, maybe I will once I close out everyone's tabs." Sharla shrugs and turns to face me. "Want me to carry your clothes downstairs and start them in the wash?"

Is she their maid? I'm so damn confused right now. "Um, thank you, but I won't be here long enough for all of that." I look over at Blaine as I reach for my wallet in my purse and open it. "I'll pay you for your clothes. I'll even mail them back once I'm home. Will one-hundred be enough?"

The man Blaine called Emmit chuckles before turning around and proceeding down the stairs. Both Blaine and Sharla find my words amusing as well. Sharla walks up to me. "Tara, I don't know where you're from, but you ain't there anymore sweetheart. You're in Rose City, Texas. Population, well, what you saw down there." She points to the floor, insinuating the people in the bar below us. "That's about it. The roads are flooding and unless you have a helicopter coming to save your ass, you'll be going home with someone downstairs." She leans in close and whispers in my ear, "Which I don't advise. Although most are harmless. I doubt they're you're type. So, basically, it sounds like you'll be staying here. At least for the night. Oh, and the clothes of Blaine's you're wearing? He probably spent no more than thirty-dollars max on the entire ensemble." She takes my heavy, soaked, clothes from my grasp and turns on her heel, heading downstairs.

Crossing my arms, I try to shelter my body while comforting myself. I feel the loneliness and sadness as they begin to sneak in. All I wanted to do was try and prevent Preston from public humiliation while possibly saving my own ass at the time and it's turned into this. Now? I'm in a town I've never heard of stranded by an act of mother nature? I feel my emotions overwhelm and take the best of me as I plop down defeated, onto Blaine's bed. I pull my own body inward as I curl into myself and bury my face— hiding my tears from these people I don't know as I silently begin to weep.

"So, um, yeah. Big Boy will have your car around back in

no time and I'm sure by morning we'll be able to get that tire of yours fixed," I hear Blaine tell me, his tone reeks of his uncomfortableness. But I'm too upset to even care anymore. I hear his footsteps slowly fade away as he strides down the stairs.

After a few minutes when I'm certain that I'm alone, I lift my head. It has gotten quiet downstairs, so I assume most of the patrons have already left. I shuffle through my purse looking for my compact. I must look a mess. What I wouldn't give for a hot shower and to wash my hair. When I finally locate my compact, I open it and shriek inside at the sight staring back at me. Fumbling through my purse again, I find myself desperate for something, anything that will help rid my face of these mascara-stained cheeks. I luck out and find a travel pack of makeup removal wipes. After I've successfully cleaned my face, I notice my eyes are all red and blotchy from all the crying I just did.

"Well, well. Aren't you the picture of vanity," Sharla states, startling me before walking over to me as she makes herself comfortable taking a seat next to me. "I'm only teasing," she assures me, but I'm not sure I'm convinced.

I feel my inner snarky side debating on making an appearance, and she does. "Look, I know you all think I'm some uppity bitch and all I care about is money and my appearance, but you're all wrong." Now I feel the tears as they beckon to be released and slowly they begin to fall once more. "All I wanted to do was drive and take a couple of days *away* from all the people you're stereotyping *me* to be. I just wanted two whole days to myself without someone having any expectations of me." I'm not lying, but I'm not being completely honest here, either. "You know, without having my mother and father playing director of my day-to-day life. Most importantly, to spare my boyfriend the embarrassment when I publicly decline his proposal in front of the governor and hundreds of other people." That last sentence slips out with several tears as my tone lowers to nearly a whisper.

Brushing the tears away from my cheeks with my hand, I glance up at Sharla whose lips have parted at my full-disclosure declaration. She opens her mouth to speak and it's interrupted by the clearing of Blaine's throat. We both look in his direction. "Your, uh, car is safely parked in the back now." I stand in excitement and again reach for my wallet, but Blaine interrupts my search. "He's gone now. You don't owe him any money, either."

"Well. Your ma has Jett and since the roads are bad, looks like I'm stuck for the night here too. Should've asked Big for a ride, but I know he doesn't allow passengers. It's too late to call now and explain to Jett why I won't be there tonight. Ugh, I miss my baby. I hate being away from him. Want me to get the downstairs sofa ready for her to sleep on?" she asks Blaine. "Em has some extra blankets in his room." Wait. Emmit has his own room here, too? Is this seriously how these two live? I've yet to see a shower or kitchen. And Sharla has a son. The curious part of me wants to know who his father is. I mean are these three siblings? There's some strange protective vibe between them, but I can't peg exactly what it is.

"Nah." Blaine shakes his head. "She can have my bed and I'll take the recliner in Emmit's room. You can take the sofa," he tells her approaching his dresser, retrieving some boxer briefs for himself. I quickly turn away, but it's too late as the mental image of him wearing only those sends a warm tingling feeling from my stomach, falling and eventually landing between my thighs. I cross my legs pleading with my body to stop betraying me.

Wait. I just realized that this man I literally just met has assigned himself the sole decider of where I'll rest my head for the night? "Um, Sharla. All of you have been extremely nice to me. How about I take the sofa. You've worked all night and I'm sure you're exhausted. Maybe you'd prefer the bed?" Having heard myself say those words out loud, I shock myself that I'm not putting up more of a fight about all of this. This isn't exactly the five-star hotel I had in mind, but it's been a long day and I am exhausted. Yes, that must be it. It's just one night, not the rest of my life.

"Yeah. That's gonna be a hard pass from me, but thanks.

Blaine's like a brother to me and I'd rather not sleep in the same bed he's fucked every woman in town, including my arch enemy." She shifts her gaze to him just in time to meet his and I watch his eyes narrow, gloss over, as his glare causes me to shudder. "What? It's only the truth. It's still early for me anyway. It's only midnight. If I'm gonna be stuck here for the night, may as well make the best of it." She turns on her heel and heads downstairs, leaving me all alone with the man who saved me tonight. Five minutes ago I hadn't necessarily thought of anything but Blaine's hard body and what it's been doing to mine, my flat tire and trying to get out of here. Now? I find my thoughts skipping around wondering just how many women this small town hero has bedded. Oddly enough, I find myself mildly jealous of those women. Sure, he exudes sex appeal, but he also radiates with self-confidence. So much so, that it borders cockiness.

So, Blaine's not her son's father. Maybe Emmit is. Her statement doesn't make me at all comfortable given that they expect me to sleep on his bed. I look back over my shoulder as I visually scan his bed and can feel the disgust as it paints my face. "You want the fucking couch, fancy pants?" His agitated voice echoes from across the room while he takes a not so subtle jab at me. Fancy pants? Wow.

What the hell did I do? "Excuse me?" I ask, cocking my head to the side as my hand finds my hip.

"Look, just cut the shit. I see the way you looked at my bed and, well, basically everything I own. You drive a fucking Lexus and that purse of yours ain't cheap. You're not from around here, but you have Texas plates. I heard your little admission earlier. Oh, poor little rich girl." He waves his hands around in the air, and he's honestly a little scary right now. I'm either naïve or confused at why he seems so upset. "So, your wealthy boyfriend was gonna propose to you in front of a ton of other rich people including the governor? What a fucking problem to have." He unbuttons his jeans without stopping his admonishing of me. Suddenly, I'm distracted by his actions as my eyes now follow his jeans all the way to the floor. My body begins reacting again to the sight of this man and I find it infuriating. I'm not entirely sure what this feeling is and maybe it's the exhaustion and conflicting emotions ruling me and my body. But I find myself wishing he would scoop me up with those rugged manly hands of his and do downright filthy things to my body with them. What would his lips feel like on mine? His flesh on mine as he fucks me so hard that the world around me completely ceases to exist? He approaches me with an arrogant smirk on his face. I'm not sure how this man has just gone from zero to one-hundred and now back to zero? Is he off his medication or something? "See something you like, fancy pants?" He raises his hand and grazes my cheek, causing goosebumps to pebble my skin. My heart slams against the walls inside my chest and my clit begins to throb as his skin makes contact with mine. Why is my body being so disloyal? I turn my head away from him. I no longer trust myself right now. If I acknowledge him in this moment, I might end up doing something I regret in the morning. He chuckles slightly before I notice him throw a towel over his shoulder from my peripheral, along with a large bulge confined in his jeans. Christ, his cock looks massive, but I refuse to give him the satisfaction of knowing I couldn't resist stealing a look. What an arrogant asshole. "Sleep tight," he finishes before turning and leaving me alone with a worked-up body.

I fall back onto his bed as I pant, trying to catch my breath.

BLAINE

Fuck! Typically I despise wealthy people, especially women and the way they act and flaunt their material shit. Especially snobby ass women acting like a man is only worth the amount of money he has in his checking account. So, I don't know what it is about Tara that makes my cock ache to feel what it's like to be inside of her. I've fucked lots of women, but something about that woman upstairs makes me wanna explore her both inside and out. God, I wanna fuck the snooty, underlying bitch I know that lies within, right out of her. Passing by the bar, I grab a beer, pop the cap and take a long pull before I look over at the couch. Sharla's not there, but she's made a comfy-looking bed out of it. Emmit's room is in the back, downstairs.

"Yo, Em." I tap my knuckles against his door before pushing it open. I'm engulfed in a cloud of smoke. "What the fuck, man?" I wave my arms around, clearing the air some. Like two deer in headlights, Sharla and Emmit both stare back at me with lit cigarettes in their hands. This wouldn't be shocking if it were just my brother. He smokes. Sharla on the other hand, does not. I scan the room and notice a bottle of whiskey sitting between them. "Since when the fuck do you smoke?"

"Since…now?" Sharla smirks as she takes a drag and blows out a ring of smoke, intentionally trying to piss me off. I approach her and before I can yank it from her, Emmit stands, challenging me. "You fucking serious, Em? You're encouraging this shit?"

Sharla finds her feet and places herself in between the both of us. "Look, I appreciate you always having my back and feeling the need to protect me…but I'm grown,

Blaine." She shifts her eyes to the beer in my hand. "Oh, I get it now." She turns to Emmit. "He might've finally met a woman who won't fuck him and he's coming in here taking his pent-up aggression out on me. This is way deeper than me smoking a fucking cigarette." She turns her eyes back to me and bats my chest. "Did you lay your best moves on her and she rejected you? Christ, Blaine. I'm glad she didn't fall under whatever spell it is these women do when they meet you. Your ego has been out of control for a while now. Plus, that woman has been through some serious shit. The last thing she needs is for you to further complicate things."

I cock my head to the side and take another long pull from my beer. "What do you mean she's been through some serious shit? And not that it's any of your business, but I have zero desire to fuck her." I'm lying right through my front teeth. I want her, and I want her bad. "Don't tell me you feel sorry for some snobby rich chick that probably fled a mansion with servants and shit all because her filthy rich boyfriend was gonna propose? And, gasp, in front of the fucking governor. Yeah, I heard that shit. You do realize that our own mother essentially traded Emmit and I for a life of luxury and material things?"

"Blaine, why are you in here? Go fucking beat off in the shower, man. I'm your brother. You can't fucking fool me. I saw the way you've been eye-fucking her since you first saw her. She's only been here a few hours and you're already losing your shit over her. Get a hold of yourself, brother. Does anyone else find it ridiculous that we're all in here arguing over some random woman who showed up in the rain and will be gone by morning after her tire's fixed? Come on. Aside from our team winning state tonight, this shit's been weird." Emmit pours himself a shot and slams it back.

"True. All of it. I'm in agreement with Em," Sharla replies, acknowledges Emmit. "Is that all you heard from her though, Blaine? The part about her leaving because of her boyfriend?"

Puzzled by her question, I can feel the lines on my forehead crinkle as I arch a brow. "Yeah. And it's typical rich bitch drama."

"I actually like her and feel something genuine about her. But, since she'll be leaving, I decided not to invest myself any further into her. Wow, Blaine. I thought you were like the fucking pussy-whisperer and shit. It turns out, you can't read a woman as well as we all thought." Sharla takes the shot of whiskey Emmit's poured for her and swallows it down. Sharla's always been like a sister to us, but I'll be damned if she doesn't act like another brother sometimes with the things that leave her mouth.

"Eh, you're fucking wrong about her. They're all the same.

Money does shit to people. She's no exception. I'm going to shower," I tell them. "I'm ready for bed. Ready for this night to be over. So, if you don't mind?"

"Take the couch, ya big grouch. I'll sleep in here tonight," she fires back.

"Fine." I turn my back to them both and walk out.

CHAPTER FOUR

TARA

Trapped in this room, I am a prisoner of my own making as I pace the floor. I should just make a call to my father and have him send a helicopter or rescue team for me. For a fleeting moment, I debate the thought on a serious note. No. Then this entire ordeal that I've submitted myself to would be in vain. Pausing, I look down at Blaine's clothes that I'm currently wearing. God, they smell so good as I take a long whiff of his scent. It's so manly and natural. So different than what I'm used to, and it ignites another fire inside of me—leaving me longing for what exactly I'm unsure, as I stand here and burn slowly with its flames. Sure, he's easy on the eyes but clearly, we come from two different worlds. Oh, the audacity he had to assume he knows anything about me or what I've been through.

I refuse to let another man, especially one that knows next to nothing about me spew that vitriol in my face as I sit idly by. Sure, he and his family have been nice enough to let me crash here, and while I'm grateful, I have to let him know just how wrong he is about me.

Throwing caution to the wind, and possibly risking my own life as I don't honestly know these people, I march loudly down the stairs. Once I'm at the bottom, I see Blaine laying on the sofa. Not what I expected to see at all. Another heat wave crashes through my body when I notice he's only wearing his boxer briefs. Well, genius, what are you going to do now? The sight of him has proven over and over again to make you weak, longing for him inside. He's asleep and I'd look like a mental patient for sure if I woke him only to shout at him about things he said to me hours ago. I feel my mouth begin to water and myself become suddenly wet the more I gaze at his perfectly formed body. Christ don't get me started on that tattoo on his chest and shoulder. That sort of thing is considered taboo where I come from. Is that what this is? Blaine is so different than any of them and internally it's grinding every gear inside of me. Get a hold of yourself,

Tara. This isn't like you at all. I've only ever slept with one man, but I can't help but wonder what kind of sexual beast Blaine would be between the sheets. Quickly, I try to shake him out of my thoughts and I shift my gaze to a half empty bottle of vodka sitting on the counter of the bar. Fuck it. If I'm going to rid myself of these thoughts and have a shot at any sleep tonight, I'm going to need some of this.

"I'll ask again. See something you like?" Blaine's deep and unexpected voice booms throughout the room, causing me to jump where I stand.

I thought he was asleep. Oh please don't let him have caught me drooling over him. It seems like this man already gets enough of that attention from other women. Clearing my throat, I square my shoulders ready to defend myself. "I couldn't sleep and thought maybe a drink might help. Of course, I would pay for it, though. I wasn't trying to steal or just help myself to your liquor."

He throws his feet over the side of the sofa until they touch the floor. Oh dear god, please don't let him stand and approach me. He places his hands between his legs and on his cock, adjusting himself and without shame before he stands. My gaze is fixated on the enormous swelling that remains and it takes all the will power I have to peel my eyes away from it. "Well, help yourself. It's on the house." He's now behind the bar and I hear the clinking of glass.

"I know that where you probably come from, everything has a price." He sets not one, but two shot glasses on the counter. "Around here though, not everything has a price tag on it. It's called generosity. Doing something good just for the sake of doing so. Even if that something is as small or simple as a few shots. Now, go ahead. Someone else playing bartender for once? I might like this."

I swallow thickly as I try to process his words. He's not being a complete asshole. Not yet anyway. My eyes slowly trail down his bare chest as far as they can before I snap myself out of it again. I simply nod and pour the clear liquor into each shot glass. He takes his and I follow his lead. He raises his glass and eyebrows before throwing his head back along with the drink. I do the same and the burn as it slides down my throat causes me to cough before I wipe my mouth with the backside of my hand. "Wow. That was rough."

"Nah," he replies, taking the bottle from me before he pours another round of shots for us.

"Woah, woah. I don't think I can handle any more of that. I was only going to take one shot anyway." He smirks at my reply. His mischievous grin combined with the dimple that's now accentuated, has my core yearning for him again.

"Just one more." He slides the glass across the wooden

countertop in my direction. "The second one won't be as rough. Promise."

Is he trying to get me drunk? I am a lightweight, but he doesn't know that. One damn shot and I'm already a little buzzed. This version of him compared to earlier has me feeling like I could sit here for hours with him just drinking and talking. It's infuriating and leaves me frustrated and confused but fuck it. I guess I can take just one more. I raise my glass, but instead of taking the shot I quickly put it back down still full and watch as confusion etches across his face.

"You know all those things you said to me earlier? Well, guess what?" His eyes slowly narrow and I feel my courage diminishing. Quickly I slam back that second shot and shudder before I continue. Yes, I need the help and courage the alcohol gives me. "You don't know shit, Blaine. Do I have money? More than I can spend in a lifetime. Do I idolize money and name brand items? Yeah, it's an unfortunate consequence from the way I was raised and the family I was born into. Yes, I have it on good authority to believe that my boyfriend has every intention of proposing tomorrow. Well, technically tonight I suppose." Damn, it suddenly dawns on me that it's already my birthday. "Am I running from that? Hell yes, I am! Because, Blaine, where I come from, the women are groomed from birth to *act* a certain way. To *be* a certain way. And, when we do find a worthy man we should *be* so lucky…" I hesitate briefly considering the absurdity of that reality. "A man that supposedly *loves* us and wants to marry us? *We* should be so lucky?" I shake my head. "And let me tell you, Blaine." I grab the bottle and help myself to another shot and down it quickly. This time it goes down smooth as my throat is numb. "I *refuse* to become another one of those statistics. I will not essentially become a human incubator for the next generation of elitist assholes while a nanny raises my children and my allegedly loving husband *fucks* any and every slut that throws her pussy in his face. So, if that makes me a rich bitch and all those other tacky things you said about me earlier, then I suppose you were right. But know this. The way you judged me without knowing a single fucking thing about me, is the same damn thing you claim people like me do to others who are less fortunate. The one fucking thing I want most in life I can never buy! And that's love. The kind of love that's organic and real. The kind that keeps you up late at night with goofy conversations stemming from delirium. The kind of love that keeps you on a natural high and buzz…zero alcohol required."

He stares at me for what feels like an eternity and says absolutely nothing. I feel the warmth of my cheeks as I know they begin to blush, revealing my embarrassment at my sudden lashing out. I just bared my soul and exposed my deepest truth to a complete stranger. I've never felt so vulnerable in my entire life.

BLAINE

I'VE NEVER FELT LIKE SUCH AN ASS IN MY ENTIRE LIFE. Outside of my family, I'm not sure any other woman has ever shown me such a raw and vulnerable side of them. Staring into her pain-stricken eyes as they water, I can feel her battle as if it were my own. A tear rolls down her cheek and she shies away from me as she wipes it away. I move from behind the counter and approach her, only I don't know what to do with her once I'm next to her. I'm not the lovey-dovey, hands-on, consoling type of man.

Slowly, she looks up at me and feigns a smile, attempting to shelter her vulnerability. Her eyes lock with mine. "So, yeah. That's me. The poor little rich girl who can buy anything…almost."

My fucking god I want to take her in my arms, carry her to my bed and explore every inch of her body with mine. Normally I would, but this is different, she's different. I run my hand through my hair before I feel them drag down my face. "Tara, I…" she stifles my words and cuts me off, catching me off-guard as her lips crash onto mine.

Reaching around, I tightly wrap my arm around her back and pull her in close to me. Her abdomen presses into my growing cock. I swipe my tongue across her lips and she lets out a moan. As they part, it grants my tongue the access it desperately craves. She tastes of innocence and purity. Greedily, I inhale her whimpers as I want her, all of her. My other hand roams down her backside and into those baggy sweatpants of mine she's wearing. I grab and squeeze her firm ass cheeks. Fuck I could almost come right now at the thought of burying my cock in between them. She leaps up unexpectedly and wraps her legs around my waist and her arms around my neck. I break our kiss momentarily. "Tara, you sure about this?" Her expression pleads to me, assuring me we share the same desire.

She nods quickly without hesitation before she plunges her mouth back to mine. I carry her up the stairs, into my room, and lay her on my bed. Hovering over her small frame, I look deeply back into her eyes. They tempt me to devour her and my cock agrees. She licks her lips and reaches between us and grabs my length before she begins to stroke it gently. "Oh, God. Tara." My eyes roll back in my head knowing her delicate and damn near virgin fingers are around my dick.

"Do it Blaine," she says in a whisper, encouraging me. I feel the precum dampen my boxer briefs.

This is wrong. She's all but engaged to someone else. I might fuck a lot of women, but I do not fuck another man's woman. I'm not sure I have the mental or physical strength at this point to control myself, but I have to. "Tara." I take a deep breath and top her hand with mine, pulling it from my cock. She doesn't know it, but this is taking all the willpower in me to consider not making her all mine, even if for one night. Looking up at her, I watch as her eyes shift back and forth eagerly between mine. "This is wrong."

I watch her face fall at my declaration and inwardly I condemn myself for letting it get this far to begin with. Rejection etches across her beautiful face, but nothing could be further from the truth. I want this woman more than I've ever wanted any other in my entire life. "Blaine, no it's not. Not if we both want it. I'm not drunk. Is this about…Preston?"

Ah, there it is. His name and for some reason it fucking stings when she says it. I nod, swallowing down the lump now formed in my throat. "Yes…and no."

She cups my face with those angelically soft hands. "Look at me. He and I are over."

I already figured as much technically, but he doesn't know

that. Does he deserve an explanation from her if what she said earlier is true? Fuck no. He's not worthy of her in any way. "Tara, even if I do…I can't promise you more than one night. I'm sorry. I just can't." Still holding myself up on top of her body, my head drops at my admission. As much as I want her, she deserves my honesty.

She quickly places her finger under my chin and lifts it back up. Reluctant to fall prey to her gaze, I drag my eyes back up to meet hers. "Lie to me, Blaine." She places her finger over my lips. "Don't say anything. Just show me what it would *feel* like to be yours. Please?"

I don't think she's fully prepared for what she's asking of me. As wrong as this must be, it just feels so goddamn right, and with her plea I feel my body begin to cave and do as she requests.

TARA

HIS WORDS TELL ME ONE THING, BUT HIS MENACING EYES say another. They stare back deep into mine, penetrating and undressing my entire existence, leaving me exposed and lusting for more. Blaine is a drug, and after just one passionate kiss, I'm intoxicated and addicted. My body has never in my life reacted in this way, and it would be a sin not to let him consume me with his. Smashing his lips to mine, he forces his tongue inside my mouth while they each battle to seize control. "I hope you know what you just asked for." He pulls away, breaking our connection yet again. Grabbing the hem of the t-shirt, he yanks it up over my head, exposing my breasts. Momentarily he feasts his eyes on them. Wasting no time, he cups one of them and begins to dine on it as he sucks and flicks his tongue over my erect nipple. They're so sensitive to his teeth it's a beautiful pain. I cry out, expressing my pleasure as my body comes to life beneath him. He assaults both my breasts and I can feel an orgasm stirring around in my core, making its way downward with fury. "Yes!" I cry out before I feel my teeth sink into my lower lip as my neck and back arch.

The warm wetness of his tongue slides up the flesh of my neck before he grabs the waist of the sweatpants and yanks them, lowering them down my legs. I wiggle my legs and he helps until they're removed completely. He removes his boxers and his hard cock springs free and my release threatens to explode at the sight. I watch as his eyes begin to slowly roam back up body, stopping at my pussy. Parting my legs with his knees, he stares before grabbing his cock stroking it while he looks at my assuredly glistening wet pussy. "That's the most beautiful and perfect pussy I've ever seen and I'm about to make you both remember my name." He's in complete control and a sexual beast, just as I had fantasized. The adrenaline racing through my veins is unlike anything I've ever experienced as I impatiently await his assault.

He reaches in between the mattress, confusing me momentarily before he pulls out a condom. He rips it open with his teeth and I watch as he begins to slide it on. Jealousy surges through my body fleetingly at the rubber that hugs his cock. He then positions himself lower on top of me as he holds his cock and glides it up and down my wetness, throwing his head backward on contact. Looking back at me, his eyes hold captive the beast within that silently warns and pities me. Lining himself up completely with my folds, he slowly begins to push himself inside of me. I loop my arms between his and hold onto his back. He's large and the more he pushes into me, the more I feel him stretching my walls. It burns but feels so damn good. He slowly pulls himself back out of me a little and I feel a whimper escape. I dig my nails into his back and scratch them down his bare flesh. My body beckons to have him back inside of me, and with one buck of his hips, he slams himself back in. This time I scream, expressing the pleasure of him being inside of me. Repeatedly, he thrusts in and out of me, bringing me closer to ecstasy with each buck of his hips.

BLAINE

GODDAMN SHE'S SO FUCKING TIGHT AND WET FOR ME. MY cock won't be able to take much more. She's getting close to her release. I can feel her walls as they greedily hug my cock tightly, squeezing it with each pump. I'm not gentle or slow. I don't know how to be and slowly she's beginning to adapt to the way I'm taking her. She digs, claws and scratches her way up and down my back. Her hands lower to my ass cheeks and she digs in, pushing them toward her, encouraging me to keep going. "Don't stop, Blaine!" Mercilessly, I slam in and out of her and it happens. Her pussy clamps around my cock so hard with her orgasm that it forces mine at the same time.

"Yes, Tara! Come for me, all over my dick. Ah, fuck!" I growl out, as my pumps begin to slow, and I watch her beautiful face as she rides out the final wave of her orgasm.

Sweaty, and breathless, I stare at her as I hold myself on top of her. "Blaine?" she asks, with me still inside of her.

Drops of my sweat fall onto her perfect naked body, mixing with hers. "Yeah?"

"Can we just stay like this for a minute?" she asks in a soft tone, her honey-glazed eyes weaken me, so I look away. Being inside of her still while looking at her is something I could do over and over. And, that fucking scares me.

I don't understand the reason for her request, but I comply. After a few moments, I slide myself out of her and fall over next to her on my bed.

CHAPTER FIVE

TARA

I whimper internally as Blaine pulls himself out of me. Not because I'm in love with this man but being one with him was exhilarating. It's the most alive I've felt in my entire life and I wanted to savor every second. Not to mention, he just gifted me the best birthday present. This feeling will be hard to top.

I watch as he removes the condom and throws it away. "Um, so, we do have a shower downstairs. Ya know, in case you wanted to use it." He's acting strange toward me now. He warned me, and I knew this was a one-time thing, but I suppose I foolishly allowed myself to believe he wouldn't go cold and awkward toward me in the same night. "I can take you downstairs and show you where it's at. Sharla keeps some girly stuff in there. I'm sure she wouldn't mind if you used some of it."

I'd be lying if I didn't admit a part of me feels slightly crushed inside. Did he not feel what I felt in that moment? Probably not. I must remind myself he's a playboy. This is what he's used to. I have no right to feel upset in any way. He did what I begged him to, and at least I'll always have that memory.

"Sure," I reply as I fumble around looking for his clothes I was wearing earlier.

———

AFTER BLAINE TAKES ME DOWNSTAIRS AND SHOWS ME where the shower is I hop in and let the hot water and soap wash away what was left of our shared experience. A part of me grieves that also. Blaine had a new toothbrush that he so kindly gave me to use. After I'm showered and dried off, I put the clothes back on I wore earlier. Thankfully, I have a hair brush in my purse and I'm able to comb out the tangles in my hair. Finally, I brush my teeth and rinse away the last part of Blaine that remained—his taste.

Walking out of the bathroom, I look around and listen. It's so quiet in here and strange considering it's a bar. I place my hand over my face questioning my actions and this night yet again before a small giggle escapes as I shake my head. Suppose this is one way to give my parents and the rest of Dallas' elite the middle finger. At least when I leave in the morning I can say with an honest heart that I have zero regrets.

As I enter the main area of the bar, I catch Blaine fast asleep on the sofa he was on when this entire thing started. I clutch my chest at the sight of him. He's such a beautiful man. A bit of an asshole, but beautiful nonetheless. And, he shared himself with me even if only for this night.

Once I make my way upstairs, I notice my clean, dried clothes laying over the chair he has in his room. Such a simple act of kindness and I feel my heart swell. There's more to Blaine. There's a reason why he sleeps with many women but never lets them get close enough. That chip he seems to carry on his shoulder about people of my social class must also have a story behind it. I'll never get the chance to find out the answers to these questions, but I do wish him the best.

I crawl back into his bed and curl up as my lids grow heavy and sleep soon finds me.

BLAINE

"MORNING!" MY MA HOLLERS OUT, CAUSING ME TO PRY MY eyes open. "Em, Blaine, Sharla!"

"I want Momma," the sound of Jett's tiny voice also echoes throughout the bar.

"Yep. Momma's here. And we brought Uncle Blaine and Emmit some breakfast." Through my sleepy eyes trying to focus, I watch my ma place Jett up on a barstool as she places his breakfast in front of him. "Now, let's try to find you some orange juice and then we'll get everyone in here." She looks around, scanning the condition of the bar and shakes her head before her eyes find mine. "Blaine Michael Knight. Did y'all not even attempt to clean this place after last night? Your brother's right. You really should think about hiring some more help around here," she tells me before heading behind the bar to pour Jett a glass of juice and starts making a pot of coffee.

I rub my eyes while I try to process her early morning chastising. Something catches my gaze out of my peripheral and I notice Tara shyly peeking her head around the corner from the top of the stairs before she retreats. Thoughts of last night flood my memories and I momentarily lose myself in them as I feel my heart hammer inside my chest. She's not like other women I've encountered that are wealthy. Behind those hypnotic golden orbs lies someone much deeper than money. Fuck. Just the thought of her eyes penetrating mine as she begged me to fuck her make my dick instantly hard. I place the blanket over my lap, covering my hard-on.

Suddenly, Emmit and Sharla walk out of his room and both have huge smiles plastered on their faces as they giggle while whispering to one another. I know that look on my brother's face. I know that smile and the way he's looking at her. They slept together!

"Momma!" Jett screams, climbing off the barstool before running up and into his mother's arms.

Sharla looks surprised for a second, but instantly embraces her son while planting kisses all over his face while he giggles.

I cast my judgmental gaze toward Emmit who is already eyeballing me, but he immediately looks away and heads toward our ma. He leans down and gives her a hug before she pulls breakfast out and places it in front of him on the bar. "Sit. Eat." She pats the counter in front of him. "You too, Sharla." My ma turns back to me. "Come on Blaine, come and eat," she orders me, but I need a minute to let my stiffy go away.

"Ma, I'm in my boxers."

Sharla turns in my direction. "I'll run upstairs and grab you some pants if ya want? Check on Tara, too. She still here or has she left?"

"So, that's whose fancy car is parked out back? I was wondering who that belonged to. Is she here? Tara?" my ma chimes in, causing me to scrub my face with both my hands. The last fucking thing I need is for her to have knowledge or add her two cents into this. For now, the only people who know what happened last night are Tara and me. I'd like to keep it that way, too.

"Will these work?" Tara asks, unfazed as she plays it cool walking down the steps holding out a pair of jeans for me.

There she is. Dressed and absolutely breathtaking. Last night before I fell asleep, I found myself feeling different about her than I have about any other woman. But, I told myself that when morning came that the feeling would've subsided. It hasn't and if anything, being in close proximity again is proving that and I hate it. My heart picks up in pace the closer she gets to me and I fight relentlessly to control my dick from growing again. She hands the jeans to me, sets her purse down on the sofa and grins before turning her back to me and walking up to my ma.

I stand still managing to cover my dick while I slip into my jeans and watch Tara at the same time. "Hi. I'm Tara." She extends her hand delicately and my ma reciprocates the gesture.

"I'm Margaret. Blaine and Emmit's mother. But you can call me Ma. Everyone else does. It's a pleasure to meet you, Tara." She looks over Tara's shoulder and makes eye contact with me before turning back to Tara. "Are you hungry, dear? I made plenty. Here, sit." She pats the bar stool.

Making my way over to them, I give my ma a hug and grab a breakfast sandwich before I walk behind the bar and pour myself a cup of coffee. Holding the glass pot up, I turn and ask, "Anyone else want a cup?" My eyes stop as they lock with Tara's. This is a mistake. I can feel myself losing the battle as I await her reply and fight to peel my gaze from hers.

"Sure," she answers me, her voice laced thick with hesitation. She turns to my ma. "Thank you so much, Margaret, for the offer. But I already put a call in to have a tire delivered and changed. They should be here shortly. A cup of coffee should be enough to get me going." I listen and watch as Tara goes back and forth with my ma. Sliding the mug of coffee over to Tara, I set creamer, sugar, and a spoon in front of her considering I have no clue how she takes her coffee.

"Nonsense," my ma replies. "Sit and eat."

"Nothing's better than our ma's famous breakfast sandwich," Emmit states through a mouthful of food. He's not wrong. "A homemade croissant, ham, bacon, egg, topped with cheese. It's kinda famous around these parts."

She looks up and catches me watching her. She has a look of desperation and confusion on her face. Her phone rings, giving her the excuse she looked like she needed to avoid any further conversation with my ma. She rushes over to her purse, retrieving and answering her phone. I watch her from afar until Sharla loudly taps the bar counter, pulling me from my haze. "Hey stargazer. Can I have a minute with you in private, please?" she asks through somewhat gritted teeth before standing and walking toward the back. Ma looks at me with curious eyes and I shrug before heading toward Sharla.

"You do realize she's about to leave, right?" Sharla firmly plants her hands upon her hips.

"Yes. Your point being?" I retaliate.

She rolls her eyes at me. "Blaine. Seriously. I've known you almost my entire life. I know you haven't been the same after Natalie and that's understandable. But, since that woman out there walked into this place last night you've been an entirely different person. Shit, I watched the visual exchanges between the two of you. The way you both kept undressing one another with your eyes. One night, Blaine. It's only been one damn night and the change in you is already apparent. Even I have to admit that it's a good look on you. I think she's into you, Blaine. And by the way things sounded last night, you were defi- nitely into her." She folds her arms over her chest. Her revelation proves that my little secret is not in fact a secret. "You're too afraid to admit it to yourself out of fear that you're gonna let her just walk right out of your life? Maybe it's for the best. I might be like a sister to you, but sometimes you're a real fucking jerk. Something more than sex happened between the two of you. Because the Tara I briefly spoke to sounded as if she was not only running, but in search of something. So, she either revealed something about herself to you, causing you to think differently about her. Or, you just lucked out. Considering the last time Emmit and I spoke with you, you were upset and angry, treating me more like a child than a friend. My guess is the former."

"You don't know shit, Sharla. How about I dissect you and how I know judging by the shit-eating grins you and Em were sporting this morning that the two of you slept together?" I retaliate as I point toward Emmit's bedroom. "This is crucial as it has the potential to affect all of our lives. Not to mention this bar. How could y'all be so careless?"

"No." She shakes her head at me. "You're not gonna deflect this onto me. The difference here being that I do have actual feelings for Emmit and can admit it. But this is how self-absorbed you are, Blaine. Emmit and I have been dancing around each other for years. Doing what you're doing with Tara after just one night. The spark between the two of you is…almost palpable. In all my years I've never seen you look at *any* woman the way you have at her. Give yourself a possible chance, Blaine. Emmit and I finally caved and accepted that what we feel for one another isn't just superficial. It's always been underlying, we were both just too scared to admit it. Even if all you do is exchange your number with her, you have to take a risk starting *somewhere*. I'm not saying Tara is or isn't the one for you. But everyone deserves to love and be loved unconditionally. Now, I've said what I needed to and I'm going back in there with my son and Emmit."

TARA

I thanked Emmit and Margaret for their hospitality, but Sharla and Blaine were nowhere to be found. I figured it was probably for the best considering I never planned on feeling the way I did after we slept together. I fooled myself into believing I could have a single night with him without any expectation afterward. Maybe it's because I've never done anything like that before in my life? It gave me a sense of freedom that money has never given me. Alongside the most mind-blowing orgasm I've ever experienced in my life. For that, I will be grateful.

As I cruise down the freeway I realize that my phone hasn't gone off once today. Shocking considering I figured my parents would've already sent a search party or something to look for me. And the fact that it's my birthday and not even Carmen has called or texted me? I exit the highway and pull into the nearest gas station. Once I'm stopped, I fumble through my handbag searching for my cell. Frantic, I begin to look under my seats and in the back floorboard. No, no, no. Please God this can't be happening. I will look so desperate and pathetic if I go back now. But I fear I might just have to do that. I could always go inside this gas station and ask to use their phone to call the bar and ask Sharla to bring it out to me without anyone knowing. But what if Blaine or Emmit answer?

After devising my plan, I step out of my car and square my shoulders while telling myself I can do this. I enter the gas station and blow out a sigh of relief that the attendant is a man. Approaching the counter, the man looks up at me. "What can I get for you?" He licks his lips while lowering his elbows casually on the counter.

I smile before letting out a small nervous laugh. Something about him is creepy and sends a chill down my spine. "You're probably going to think I'm crazy for asking this, but I need a favor."

Narrowing his eyes, he leans closer to me. Maybe this was a bad idea. "Anything for you, pretty lady," he says, still inching closer over the counter as I slowly begin to back away.

The door flies open and my eyes grow wide in both shock and relief. "Blaine? What are you doing here?"

I notice my phone in his hand, but he turns, and his eyes fixate on the attendant. "Tara, why are you stopped here?" he spits out, talking to me, but closely eyeing the man behind the counter intently.

"I-I was going to call the bar because I left my phone there." Actually, I was hoping the man wouldn't be creepy and he'd call the bar, ask for Sharla and then hand the phone to me. But, I never made it that far and now, it doesn't matter.

Blaine walks up to me and places his hand on my lower back, never taking his eyes from the man behind the counter. "Come on. You shouldn't be here," he tells me, leaving me confused at his concern for not only me, but the fact he drove around looking for me. He begins to usher me to the door and I allow it. "Put your eyes back in their sockets, Ray. This one's off limits," he finishes, pointing at the man before pushing the door open.

Have my ears just deceived me? What does he mean insinuating I'm off limits? Is he saying that I'm his? The thoughts running through my mind aren't participating in a marathon, they're sprinting. And as each one crosses the finish line, my heart rate increases, awakening the sleeping butterflies again. I stop before we make it to my car. "Blaine, how did you find me?"

He stops and hesitantly drags his eyes to mine and I notice something new inside of them. Vulnerability. "I knew you couldn't have gotten too far, so I took a chance and headed west. It's a good thing, too. That man in there? That's Ray. Jett's father. He's a piece of shit and abuses women."

"Oh. Wow. That's horrible. I realized it was a bad idea once I noticed his eyes darken and he began to lick his lips while gawking at me like a piece of meat." I reach for my phone and he places it in my hand. I debate asking him what he meant in there but decide against it. I will continue to respect his warning. "Well, thanks for going to all of this trouble. I wanted my phone back but didn't want to bother you. I promise I was going to try to leave you out of it." I feel my heart begin to sink because he hasn't said anything, and I've gone out of my way to not look desperate and now it's just getting awkward quick. "Thanks again," I tell him before I walk past him and up to the door of my car.

"Happy birthday, Tara!" he hollers out behind me, leaving me stunned as I turn around to be greeted with a grin on his face. "Oh, and I put my number in your phone," he states confidently, still wearing that grin which now appears smugger but so damn sexy.

"How did you know?" I shout back at him while he stealthily approaches me until only inches separate our bodies. "I mean…about my birthday?"

"Someone named Carmen and a few other people sent you texts wishing you a happy birthday. Yeah, I peeked at them when they rolled across the top of your phone." He leans into my ear, whispering the last part, his breath warms my flesh while causing it to tingle. I can feel my teeth sink down into my lower lip as I close my eyes while shifting my head away from him. Thoughts of him devouring my body against this car while he professes to the world that I am his consume me, leaving my panties soaked. "Don't go," he pleads softly into my ear taking me by surprise wile placing my phone back in my hand.

My eyes shoot back open and find his. "What? Blaine, I…"

He stifles my words with his. "Tara. I know I told you that I couldn't promise you more than last night. And that might be true. Fuck." He shifts backward a little while he runs his hands through his hair. "Look, I know you have a life and family in Dallas…but I also know that it's not one you're necessarily happy with. This isn't me, Tara. I don't chase women down to return phones." He chuckles beneath his breath, almost frustrated at himself. "There's something between us and I've felt it since the first time our eyes met. You tell me I'm wrong and I'll drive away now."

I swallow thickly as I look up into his defenseless baby-blues and shake my head. Looking down at my phone, I search his number and send him a text.

Me: You're not wrong…

Slowly, I raise my eyes back up to his and watch as he retrieves his own cell and reads my text. A slow, sexy, menacing grin emerges on his face. He grabs both sides of my face and leans down, smashing his lips against mine. His kiss is meaningful and firm as I melt into him. He pulls away, leaving me breathless and my lips feeling bruised. "You're not wrong, Blaine. But what if we are? You made it clear and still are that you're unsure about this. About us."

He places his hands above me resting on the top of my car, pinning me in. "Tara, is anything in life ever certain? No. All I'm saying is that after one night with you, I feel different inside. It feels good, raw, and most importantly dangerous. I've been hurt before, Tara." God the way my name flows so effortlessly off his tongue ignites and brings my body to life. "It's why I do the things the way I do. But also because I've never met a woman that was as innocent as you. And as real as you. Hell, maybe that was because you didn't have any expectations of me. So, it allowed you to be real and honest with me. That shit is so sexy. Not to mention you're the most beautiful woman I've ever set eyes on." He lowers one arm and I feel his hand squeeze one of my ass cheeks.

"Take me to One Knight Stand, Blaine," I purr into his ear. "I'll follow you."

The corner of his lips curl up into a naughty grin, alerting me to all the ways he's already planning to ravish my body. Adrenaline begins to surge through my veins and he smashes his lips to mine. "Nobody's there right now. It's Sunday and the bar's closed, too. Get that pussy ready for me, fancy pants," he warns against my lips before turning on his heel and headed to a truck I assume is his.

I hop into my car and follow him as we race our way back to the bar. This is reckless. Careless. Possibly the worst mistake of my life. Or the beginning of the one I only ever dreamed was possible.

CHAPTER SIX

BLAINE

I watch her pull up next to me in the back and she sinks her teeth into her lower lip after offering me a smirk. This is possibly the single most crazy thing I've done in life, but for her, I'm willing to take the risk. I'm ready to show her how I feel as I worship and savor her body with mine and letting one more second pass feels like an injustice. This woman deserves to be shown and told how special she is.

Hopping out of my truck, she meets me and jumps into my arms, wrapping her legs around my waist. Smashing her lips to mine causes my cock to grow instantly in anticipation. Her kiss is eager and greedy, holding me captive as I walk us in through the back door never freeing our mouths from one another. I fumble and stumble my way to the pool table before sitting her down. She pulls my shirt up and over my head, tossing it to the floor. I grab the hem of her shirt and drag it slowly up and over her head. I want to take my time as I relish every inch of her silky skin while I drag my eyes up her torso. Her beige bra is a nuisance and a barrier between her perfectly ample tits. I lean in and press my lips against her flesh as I suck and kiss my way up her collarbone and neck while I unclasp her bra from the back. The straps fall down her arms and I help take it off completely, exposing her perked nipples.

"So fucking perfect, Tara," I tell her, my words come out breathless. The sight of her alone nearly leaves me speechless. She moans out as I take her nipples in between my fingers, playing and tweaking them while I bite down and sink my teeth into her shoulder.

Making my way lower, I place soft kisses downward until my mouth makes contact with her breasts. I lick and suck on each one while undoing her jeans. She slowly falls backward onto the felt of the pool table and I remove her pants and find myself shocked that the thong she wore last night is missing. "Tara? Your panties?"

Raising her head she tells me, "In my purse." She shrugs. "They didn't get washed, so I went without them."

I want to punish her by fucking her hard. So hard. She

was out in the free world with nothing but some denim separating this pussy and one accidental rip away from exposing what I'd just had. What's mine! Oh, I'm gonna make her come so many times and make her scream out my name until it's the *only* thing she remembers.

Removing my own jeans and boxers, I give my cock the freedom it begs for. She tries to sit up more and I only allow her a brief peek before I gently push her backward. "Lay back, Tara. I'm gonna give you everything you want plus some. Let's see what *you've* got for me."

Parting her thighs, I stare momentarily at her glistening pink folds before I bend down, tracing them lightly with my tongue. She squirms immediately as my tongue makes contact. Up and down her opening I glide my tongue until I slide my tongue inside her pink warmth before I pull it back out. "Blaine. Oh, I can't…"

The assault from my tongue on her pussy drives her wild as she bucks her hips into my mouth. Looking up at her is a beautiful thing to watch as I know I'm quickly bringing her to the edge before I switch it up. Nibbling on her clit, I slide one finger, then another as I finger fuck her, milking her g-spot as I hook my fingers and watch her arch her body. "Yes! Blaine!" she calls out my name for the first time. She's close to coming and I want it, I want to taste her, all of her. Removing my fingers, I shove my tongue back inside of her while I pinch and rub her clit with my fingers. I watch her body begin to tense as she also becomes more restless and I order her, "Do it. Let it go, Tara." Her sweet juice fills my mouth, treating my taste buds to her sweetness as she releases moans and whimpers before I feel her body go limp.

"I'm not done with you. We're just getting started." I pull on her legs, bringing her closer to me making access for my entrance easier. Lining my cock up with her opening, I slide it up and down the wetness of her lips as I stroke my cock before I push forward, slowly sinking into her. She cries out softly as I grip her thighs, while pumping in and out of her. Her body begins to move with mine as her tight walls hungrily suck my cock back into her each time I try to pull it out to the tip. "Move to the middle of the table," I order her as I reluctantly pull all the way out of her. She scoots her body until she's in the middle. I climb back on top of her and glance into her amber-colored eyes as they beckon and taunt me, daring me to finish what I started. I pin her arms above her head with one of my hands and she responds with a mischievous grin. She spreads her legs eagerly for me. Using my other hand I align my cock back up with her soaking wet pussy before plunging back into it. She arches her head while rewarding me with yet another whimper. Continually I pump in and out of her as she swivels her hips and matches me thrust for thrust.

"Oh, God, Blaine! Yes! I'm going to come," she warns. So, I slow my pumps, restricting her release.

"Not yet, fancy pants." I lower my hand down between her thighs and circle, pinch, and tug on her clit before I begin to increase my pace again. Lowering my head, I trail my tongue up her abdomen and circle her perfect navel with my tongue before I continue on to her breasts. Releasing her arms, I cup one of her perfect tits as I dine on a mouthful of their perfection. Sucking on each breast, I tug on her nipples until my teeth graze one and, causing her to cry out, "Yes!" I nip at it and she calls out my name repeatedly beneath me as her walls clutch around my cock and I can feel my own orgasm about to erupt. "Yes. That's it. Come for me," I command her. As her walls begin to grip my cock, they pulsate simultaneously before her release soaks my length and drips down my balls. I follow behind her, spilling my release deep inside her before my body all but falls on top of her.

Immediately, it slams into my consciousness like freight train. Not only did I not wear a fucking rubber, but I just came inside of her. I roll over next to her as we both try to catch our breath and I'm torn between the exhilaration and possible repercussions of what just happened. I certainly wasn't thinking, and I'm not sure she was either. Fuck. I glance over at her and her eyes meet mine with a smile plastered on her face. She's so fucking beautiful and happy in this moment. I don't wanna ruin it. I can't. What I feel for her is real, and selfless. But is it *selfish* or *selfless* if I don't bring this up right now?

I smile back at her and she begins to trace circles over the tattoo on my shoulder with her finger. "Did it hurt? Your tattoo?" She flickers her eyes back and forth between mine and my tattoo. Nope. I'm not saying anything about what just happened. Not in *this* moment.

"It wasn't bad." I grab her hand before I press my lips to it.

TARA

As I lay beside Blaine tracing his tattoo and still trying to catch my breath, I'm filled with this overwhelming sense of calmness. For the first time in my entire life, I've never felt so wanted and secure. Still uncertain of what exactly the future holds for us, I can't deny the connection I've felt to this man since I laid eyes on him. Only time will tell where we go from here, and I never thought in my wildest dreams I'd find this in such a small town.

"Let's shower, huh? Before we get caught with our pants

down, literally. I have no idea when Em will be back," he tells me, hopping off the pool table while offering me his hand for assistance.

I nod as I take his hand. We both gather our clothes. "I'm going to have to order some new clothes, you know?"

As we step into the bathroom, he turns the shower faucet on. "Why? You planning on staying?" he looks over his shoulder grinning.

I bat his arm. "I can go if you want?" I play along.

Quickly he turns around and his eyes go dark and sinister. "I was only teasing, Tara," he tells me, and it comes out as more of a warning than a statement.

I feel my tongue wet my lips before I suck my lower lip into my mouth. Something about the way he exudes his dominance over me, makes my heart dance erratically. "I know. I was too."

"I was serious about what I said at the gas station earlier. I don't say shit like that. Ever. We've known each other nearly one whole day, but you're doing something to me." He gestures for my hand and helps me into the shower before he climbs in behind me. Grabbing the body wash, he pours some on my back before massaging it into my skin. "I've been hurt. Same as you. That was years ago, and I promised myself I'd never let another woman in.

Never let another woman get close enough to hurt me again. And I haven't. Then there was you. Beautiful, Tara. One night with you, and everything I promised myself I suddenly found myself questioning. Sharla helped me see that. So, fuck it. I'm thirty, you're thirty." I whip around.

"How did you know my age?"

"Big Boy. He ran your plates last night. He's got some other shit on his truck, and he can basically tell me anything about anyone. He failed to tell me it was your fucking birthday today, though. I'll have to kick his ass later for that." I giggle before I grab the body wash and squeeze it over his chest. "Whoa, whoa! That's that fruity girl shit."

"Just calm down. Let me do something for you, huh? You can go outside afterward and rub against some trees or something," I tease, lathering the soap over his slick, smooth and sculpted pecs.

"God. What or who have I turned into?" I feel my lips curl up into a grin as I wash circles over him while listening to his commentary. He grabs a hold of my wrists and my eyes hastily shoot up to his. What did I do? "Tara. I'm not good at expressing my emotions considering I shut them down years ago." His eyes soften and give me that same vulnerable look from earlier. "Don't do this unless you're really willing to take this risk. Please. I don't use that word often, but for some reason still unknown to me, I'm willing to gamble with my heart where you're concerned. It seems ridiculous for me to do this, but…"

Cutting his words off with mine, I press my lips against his hand that still holds my wrist. "Blaine, this is real to me. I can't explain it either. But I'm here, and I don't plan on going anywhere."

He releases my wrists. "Tara, you will have to tie up loose ends back home. You might despise that fucking prick you were with, but you've got to end it. What about your parents? How will they feel about this? What about the rest of your family?"

He's right. I need to properly face Preston and end things once and for all. My parents will probably die on the spot from heart attacks. My sister, too. But Carmen? She'll be the only one who supports me. My old friends? Fuck them. They're all fake and only care about the latest fashion trends and gossip within our circle. "They've called and texted. And you're right. I need to inform everyone. I expect nothing less than their scrutiny and shock. They'll probably disown me, but Blaine, I don't care. This isn't some experiment for me. I've been done with what's-his-face emotionally and physically for a while now. At the end of the day, they're all willing to see me live a loveless life to keep up appearances. They don't truly care about my happiness, because if they did, they'd want what I want.

And what I want is to give this a real shot. My little sister is a lost cause. She's ten years younger than me. So, she didn't witness the earlier years in my parents' marriage when all they did was argue over my father's numerous infidelities."

"Wait. You have a sister?" he questions me, sounding shocked.

I feel a brow arch. "Is that a problem? You like younger women or something?" I feel my insecurity crawl in unexpectedly and rear its ugly head. I'm not a jealous person by nature, but Preston did a number on me.

He shakes his head. "No. Fuck no. I guess we're still learning about each other." He chuckles. "It's safe to say we're doing this completely backwards."

I cup his face, forcing his unsure, beautiful aqua eyes to meet mine. "Who says this isn't how we're supposed to do it? This is our story. We decide how we tell it and define it. I'm tired of predictable, boring 'normal' shit. Blaine, I like how this is unfolding. I like us." I lean forward, gently pressing my lips to his before he wraps his arm around the back of my head, tangling his fingers in my wet hair.

Our kiss is rough as we both fight to steal the oxygen from one another while exchanging it back and forth. Mumbled voices only growing louder by the second catch us off-guard as they echo around us outside the bathroom.

"Tara! Tara Elizabeth Billings, I know you're in here!"

I feel my eyes grow large as my heart thunders inside my chest when I realize it's my mother's voice followed by my father's.

"Your folks?" Blaine scrubs his face with his hands as I nod. "Fuck. I left the backdoor unlocked."

I fumble out of the shower and dress myself quickly as they continue to call out for me. I know they've seen my car in the back. Blaine scrambles to step into his jeans and pull his shirt over his head. "I-I'll go out first," I tell him, and am met with immediate displeasure etched on his face.

"I don't fucking think so. You think I'm gonna let you go out there by yourself and let them run over you?" He opens the door before I can answer.

I follow closely behind him, but my nerves invoke waves of nausea. "You must be Tara's mom and dad?" Blaine approaches them from behind as they scan the stairway and Blaine's side. My mother jumps and my father abruptly swings around and the color in both of their faces drain.

They dissect Blaine visually in disgust and ignore him completely before turning to me. My mother races past

Blaine and pulls me into her. "Tara, darling! You're okay! We have been worried sick."

"Please, Tara. Tell me you haven't done anything here you'll live to regret? Katherine call Preston and tell to pull over. We're taking our daughter out of this disgusting place. She needs to be seen by a doctor." My father walks past Blaine but intentionally bumps shoulders with him.

Blaine snaps. "Watch it, old man! Don't forget you're an uninvited guest at this point. Now, you can speak with your daughter with some respect, or leave. I won't ask again."

My father ignores him long enough to slide my mother aside and he grips my arm tightly, causing me to wince out in pain. "Ouch, Daddy!"

BLAINE

EVERYTHING FROM THIS POINT ON SEEMS TO HAPPEN AT warp speed. Instantly, I wrap my arm around the back of her father's neck and squeeze. He claws and pulls at my arm, but I can't seem to let go. He just hurt Tara. Both women are screaming, begging me to stop and once I drag him far enough away from Tara, I release him. He turns around and takes a swing, but I lean back, and he misses. "You don't want this, old man. I promise. Leave. Now!"

Tara stands in place as her eyes go back and forth between her parents and me while her mother rushes to her father to check on him. I walk back over to Tara to check on her. "You okay?"

She folds her arms over her chest. "Did you really have to hurt him?" She avoids looking at me, leaving me baffled and pissed.

Her father turns around. "Are you spreading your legs for this piece of trash? You have a man like Preston Hallister, and you're out here shacking up with this filth?"

My blood boils and begs my temper to erupt volcanically at his words, but I glance at Tara and watch her eyes go dark and cold. She begins to approach him, and I stay close by her, but another unfamiliar voice booms throughout the room, stopping us both.

"She's what?" A blonde haired preppy boy wearing slacks and a button-up covered by a cardigan appears. That's it. If this motherfucker says one wrong word, I'll drop him where he stands. Instinctively, I step in front of Tara. She grips the back of my shirt. "Tara, lovebug. What are you doing out here and at this dump?" He steps closer and reaches for her, but I can feel her bury her face into my back.

"Stop right there, you preppy prick. Ask the old man over there," I warn, watching his every move, ready for anything.

He chuckles at my words. "Get your filthy hands off my girlfriend, trash. She's not yours, she belongs to me." I can feel my veins constrict and my fists ball up at this mother-fucker's declaration.

"Who the fuck are these people?" Emmit's voice roars throughout the bar. Behind him are Sharla, and my ma.

"Uninvited is what they are. They're just leaving," I tell my brother.

Tara lets go and pulls away from me, stepping beside me. Emmit and Sharla stand out of the way, but to the side of Tara's family and us. My ma walks up to Tara. "You okay, honey?"

Tara doesn't answer, her eyes are firmly locked onto this Preston character. I can feel her body tremble next to mine. "Everybody shut the fuck up!" The entire bar goes silent in shock. She turns to her parents. "Mom, I know you can't help that you are who you are. So, I'll forgive you for choosing money over your happiness. That's your choice, but it isn't and will never be mine. And Daddy? You're a disgusting pig! You've been having affairs since I can remember! Not to mention you hold it over Mom's head any chance you get. So, how dare you come in here and judge one fucking thing I've done! What? You think I don't know?"

"Tara Elizabeth! You don't sound very ladylike right now!" her mother admonishes her unexpected behavior.

"Oh please, Mom! Is it ladylike to spread your legs for a man after he openly cheats in your face simply because you don't want to lose the material things you have? Or, God forbid your reputation in a society filled with complete hypocrites who are living and doing the same damn thing?"

"She's either on drugs, or needs to be committed," her father says, turning to her mother. Pointing his finger at me, he says, "this isn't over. I'll ruin you. Every last one of you!" He casts his menacing gaze at each of us. "Come on, Katherine." He grabs Tara's mom by the arm as tears spill from her eyes and pulls her out of the bar.

"If I never see you again it will be too soon!" Tara screams with balled tight fists at her side.

"Lovebug?" I can feel my eyes as they narrow at this shithead's tone and term of endearment as he begs for Tara's attention. "You're tired. Let's get you back home and have a proper doctor look you over. These people aren't your kind, Tara. You're better than this. Now let's go," he says, lunging toward her, and immediately I place her back behind me.

"Oh hell no, you prissy fuck! I will kick your ass!" Sharla roars and charges toward him but Emmit quickly wraps his arms around her as she squeals and tries to break free.

Tara steps back beside me defiantly, and it infuriates me. This bastard doesn't deserve to even set eyes on her, let alone have any chance at getting his hands on her. I *will* kill him. I know this is her moment. Her time to unleash on him everything she's been holding in, so I'll allow her that. Hopefully this asshole knows his place and keeps his hands and derogatory comments to himself.

Tara steps closer to him and I stay so close to her our arms touch. "I'm not your fucking *lovebug!* You're right, I probably am tired considering all I've done since being here is fuck *his* brains out." She shifts quickly and grabs my face, pulling me to her and firmly presses her lips to mine. For a fleeting moment I feel myself beginning to lose control as I fall under the spell of her taste, but she pulls away and we both look back to a speechless Preston. I'm not sure if I feel a sense of pride or like I've just been used. Either way, she can claim my lips with hers any damn time. In fact, if this is what being used feels like, I'll welcome it all fucking day long. "Don't look so surprised, asshole. I only wish I'd known of your infidelities sooner, so I could've found Blaine earlier. At first, I was distraught and heartbroken. Little did I know you did me a favor. We're done, and we've *been* done. Oh, and you're right. These aren't my people! I honestly don't feel I deserve the friendship and hospitality they've shown me. I've never met a group, a family, of nicer people than these right here." She points around the room at us.

"You can't be serious, Tara? Your sister was a one-time thing. It didn't mean shit to me," he tells her, shifting his feet as he pleads with her.

Her fist connects with his nose before I can blink, and instantly I wrap my arms around her, turning her away from his front and my back toward him. I don't know this fucker's temperament and I can't chance him laying a single finger on her. She squirms and hollers as she tries to break free. "Sharla! Ma! Take her upstairs, now!"

"Fuck you, Preston! The only trash in here is you! Get the fuck out! Forget I exist!" she screams as my ma and Sharla take each of her arms and escort her upstairs.

"Bitch broke my nose!" this prick declares, shocked as he holds his nose and blood pours from it, dripping onto his fucking ugly ass princess-pink cardigan.

"Now you're really gonna need a plastic surgeon!" I roar, before balling my fist and landing a shot of my own, knocking him backward and onto his ass.

"Blaine! Chill!" Emmit jumps in front of me. "This asshole doesn't deserve any more of your energy, brother."

"Get up, fucker! You heard Tara. Get the fuck out before this gets any worse!" I step closer, but Emmit places his palm on my chest.

He stumbles several times and it takes all the willpower inside of me not to beat this motherfucker within an inch of his life. "Fucking bunch of thugs! White trash, thugs! You've messed with the wrong people," he warns as he finds his feet and begins to walk away.

"Your threats don't scare me, punk! Whatever you think you can do to me, I promise I will do back ten times worse!" I growl loudly, while my brother approaches me, encouraging me to calm down. I run behind the bar and grab my gun.

"Blaine, no! Fuck!" Emmit hollers, as I chase after Preston.

When I make it to the back parking lot, he's already driving off and I fire off a warning shot, purposely missing his vehicle entirely. But, I feel the grin tug at the corner of my lips as I watch his pansy ass duck inside his little sports car. "Piece of shit!" I spit out.

CHAPTER SEVEN

TARA

My sister? Pacing the floor of Blaine's room, I clutch my sore hand. Damn that hurt but felt so good. If only I could do it twenty more times.

The loud echo of a gun being fired off startles us all and we simultaneously rush to the door trying to get through.

Sharla grabs my shoulders. "Tara, stay right here. That's exactly what Blaine would want. You know I'm right. And I know the sound of that weapon. It's Blaine's gun he keeps with him behind the bar. Ma, they're both fine. Promise. Keep an eye on her while I go get some ice for her hand and double check everyone," Sharla tells both Margaret and I, before turning on her heel, exiting the room.

I hear her words, but my heart sinks at the thought of anything happening to Blaine. I finally have a real chance at happiness and the thought of it being yanked away makes me feel weak in the knees. "Sit, dear." Margaret ushers me over to Blaine's bed where I sit. He better be okay because I can't bear the negative thoughts flooding my mind. In this moment, I feel like I could quite possibly go full-on homicidal if something's happened to him. And nothing in this moment will fulfill my need for vengeance where my ex is concerned except for beating the snot out of him and my sister. "Can you believe that shit? I knew about his slutty secretary. But, my own sister?" I look at Margaret who looks back at me with sympathetic eyes.

Margaret takes one of my hands into hers. "Tara, sweetie. We haven't really had enough time to get to know one another, but I'm so sorry. Sometimes it's our own family, our blood that betrays us the most. I can't imagine how that sort of betrayal in particular would feel, but you're better than them. That much I can tell. There will come a day that your sister will get her comeuppance and the same goes for that ex of yours." She gently pats my hand.

"Tara!" Blaine rushes into his room, and I stand before he scoops me into his arms. I nuzzle my face into his chest as tears of relief and rage build inside me before I allow them to spill down my cheeks. He squeezes me tightly while stroking my hair. "He's gone. Here, let me look at your hand." I pull out of his embrace and he wipes the tears from my cheeks with his thumb before he lifts my now swollen and bruising hand. "Let's get this ice on it. Sharla gave it to me. Ma?" He turns around to her. "Can we get a moment alone, please?" he asks, while lowering the ice pack onto the top of my knuckles and I wince out at how tender they are.

She nods. "I'll be downstairs with your brother and Sharla. Let me know if you two need anything."

"Thank you, Margaret," I reply to her generous offer.

"Sugar, I said to call me Ma. Now, you're starting to offend me. Can you just oblige an elderly woman this once?" She grins at me.

"Sure. Thank you…Ma," I honor her request although it does feel a bit odd. She turns and walks back down the stairs. Carmen. Oh, I wish Carmen were here. What will she think of me after all of this?

"Blaine is…" I begin, but he stifles my words.

"Is pretty boy shot? No. In need of a plastic surgeon, yes." He tucks a strand of hair behind my ear before walking to his dresser drawers, retrieving some medication. "Here.

Take a few of these ibuprofen for the pain and swelling. I'll go grab you a bottled water."

As I sit in here by my lonesome, I think of everything that just transpired. It's too much. I'm relieved to be away from my family and especially Preston, but it still stings. Have they no shame whatsoever? Foolishly I suppose I allowed myself to believe that none of them could stoop any lower.

"Here you go, fancy pants." Blaine hands me a bottle of water. My heart swells inside my chest when he calls me that. I open it and take the pills he gave me. "I know now is not the ideal time for food, but as far as I remember you haven't eaten today. So, while I won't exactly force you to eat yet, just know that you will be getting some calories in at some point today."

My eyes begin to water, summoning tears and one by one, they roll down my cheeks. Blaine sits down beside me, wrapping his arm around me. I lean into him. "I just want to rest right now. I'm emotionally and mentally exhausted from all the madness earlier. I'll be okay. I just feel like a nap right now."

He presses his lips to the top of my head as he softly speaks into my hair, "Rest for now. I'll lay here with you if you want?"

I reciprocate by placing a kiss on his cheek. "Please?"

He helps get me comfortable on his bed before curling up into my body from behind. The gentle caress of his fingers through my hair lulls me into a peaceful slumber.

BLAINE

ONCE I KNOW TARA'S DRIFTED OFF, I TUCK THE COVERS IN and around her small frame before heading downstairs. Sharla and Em are sharing a beer at the bar. I glide my hand across the wooden countertop as I make my way to them and plop down on a stool next to my brother.

"Care for a cold one?" he asks, after taking a pull from the glass bottle in his hand. Sharla's inquisitive eyes peek around him, meeting mine.

"Yeah, man." I scrub my face before letting out a deep and heavy sigh.

"I got it." Sharla places her hand on my brother's shoulder before making her way around the bar. She grabs my usual go-to brew and pops the cap, handing it to me. "How's she doing?"

I take several large gulps before I tell her, "Sleeping now. That was some crazy shit, man." I take another long pull from my beer. "Damn, she wasn't lying about her ex. What a piece of work. What kind of man cheats? Especially, when you have a woman like that upstairs?" I point upward to my room.

My brother pats my shoulder. "Welcome to the club of 'catching feelings' Blaine. It's a select group of elite men who were once afraid of being hurt again. I know it's early on for the two of you, but I have a good feeling about this one," he tells me as if he's sharing a hidden treasure and wealth of knowledge with me.

Propping my leg up on the bottom of his barstool, I feel my brow arch as I ask him, "And since when did you become such a master at love and feelings? And when have you ever felt the wrath a woman can leave on your heart?"

"I'd like to know the answer to this one, too," Sharla inquires, leaning in while resting her elbows on the counter.

Emmit takes a drink from his beer. "I've experienced… heartache," he shyly admits.

"Oh. No. You're not talking about Bethany from your sophomore year in high school, are you? Come on, Em. That was puppy-love at best. What did it last? All of a month?" I inquire, as the flicker of Sharla's lighter catches my attention. I watch her light a cigarette while her eyes burn holes through Emmit.

"Two, actually. And so what?" He stands. "It's true. I really liked her. Until that running back Jason transferred to our school."

"Oh, please." Sharla brushes him off with a gesture of her hand before she flicks her ash into the ashtray. "Emmit Wayne Knight that was your first piece of ass." She glares at him before her eyes soften. "Are you saying that she took your virginity and you caught feelings?"

"If that's what you wanna call it." He yanks the cigarette from her fingers, pulling a long drag before blowing out a ring of smoke. "I'm just saying, I really liked her, but the second someone new came along, that bitch dropped me like Jason did the football at our last game. Costing us the championship."

Sharla puts her smoke out and makes her way around to Emmit. "Aw. If it makes you feel better, I heard he gave her a nasty case of herpes. You dodged a bullet, babe. The way I see it, Jason delivered that little dose of karma and by doing so it allowed us to have this chance. I mean, I've gotta be honest, I wouldn't touch you with someone else's pussy if you had that shit. See how that works? Those idiots were a blessing." She rubs his shoulders before leaning around, kissing his cheek.

"Oh, Blaine. Ma's making dinner tonight. Eight o'clock sharp," Emmit informs me.

I nod my head. "Yeah, Tara really needs to eat. Wanted her to get a few hours of rest first."

"Ehem," Sharla clears her throat. "Speaking of dinner and appetites, I ordered a new pool table. That, um, stain, smackdab in the middle I thought was a bit much for our customers. And since we do serve some bar food, I figured it might not necessarily be up to code, now." She eyes me.

"Fucking hell, Sharla! How much did that set us back?" I accidentally roar out.

"Ten-thousand. That includes delivery and setup. I thought it was reasonable actually," she replies, folding her arms over her chest.

"Ten-fucking-thousand-dollars for a pool table? Have you hit your fucking head? Em, did you know about this?" If this shit keeps up, I might start smoking too.

Emmit just shrugs, acknowledging he's completely unfazed as a grin forms on his face. "That was one expensive fuck." He belts out a loud chuckle and Sharla laughs alongside him.

"Oh, I see the two new lovebirds have a bag full of jokes. Did you ever think of just calling a company to come out and clean it? Or having the felt replaced?" My knuckles begin to throb from the punch I'd landed earlier, so I begin to flex my hand open and closed. It's probably throbbing now because of the rapid pace at which the blood is now coursing through my veins.

"Oh chill, Mr. Moneybags. It was so old anyway. It needed to be replaced. Have you told Tara your deep, dark secret yet?" Sharla wiggles her eyebrows at me. "Does she know you're loaded, too?"

"No. I will when I feel the time is right, and on my own terms. For fuck's sake. Don't you have a man of your own to harass?" I hiss out.

"What dark secret?" Tara's voice booms throughout the bar as she walks down the stairs toward me.

A lump forms and lodges in my throat, but I swallow it down after several tries. Every time I see her, she absolutely takes my breath away. "It's nothing bad, fancy pants. Ma wants us to come over for dinner. It's kinda something we do since our father passed away four years ago." Smooth, Blaine. Mentally, I stroke my own ego for my quick response and ability to dodge that conversation.

She slides her arms around my lower abdomen and leans into my chest as she yawns. "I'm so sorry about your father. There's still so much we don't know about one another."

I kiss the top of her head. "Did you get a decent nap?" I can feel her nod, answering yes into my chest. "Ma only lives about ten minutes from here. If you wanna start getting ready or something, we'll be leaving here in about forty-five minutes. We really need to get some food in you."

She pulls her head back and looks up at me from under her long, shiny lashes. "I really need to call one of my personal shoppers and have them deliver me some new clothes. I can't keep wearing this for the rest of my life around here."

"The rest of your life, huh? I think I like the sound of that," I whisper into her ear, and watch her cheeks shade a bright pink. She shields her face back into my chest briefly in an attempt to hide her blushing face. Placing my finger under her chin, I tip her head back upward and kiss her forehead. "This has been the wildest damn near two days of my life, but I can't honestly say I want it any other way."

I begin to flex my hand again from the annoying throb that persists. "Let me see." Tara lifts my swollen hand up. "Looks like someone could use some ibuprofen and an icepack themselves, huh?" She softly presses her lips against the flesh of knuckles and my cock comes alive in my jeans. Fuck, this woman is gonna be the death of me. I could fuck her time and time again and it still wouldn't feel like enough.

"I'm going to grab my purse and head to the bathroom to freshen up at least." She rolls up to the tip of her toes and firmly presses her lips against mine. I can feel the low, deep growl escape from my throat. She pulls her head back and smiles at me before letting out a soft giggle. Fucking hell. Every damn thing this woman does turns my world upside down. I want to firmly plant my cock inside her and just live there. "Save that beast for later. I think I'll be ready for round three by then." She winks before turning on her heel, as she makes her way to the stairs. I watch her ass as she sways her hips side to side. It's taking every fiber in my body to restrain myself from following her up those stairs and bending her over my bed right now.

Adjusting my dick in my jeans, I turn around and notice Sharla and Emmit have disappeared. "Yo, Em. Sharla?" I call out as I approach my brother's room but stop dead in my tracks as I hear the moans and groans coming from his room. My ears. Immediately I plug them with my fingers as I flee in the opposite direction. What's been heard can never be unheard. Tara meets me at the end of the stairs. "Blaine." She grabs ahold of my arms and I pull my fingers from my ears. "What are you doing? You look like you've seen a ghost."

I shake my head. "It's worse." Her eyes grow wide with curiosity. "Sharla…and my brother. They…" I can't even finish my sentence as I reluctantly look back toward his room. Suddenly, they both come out wrapped in the same sheet and I can take no more, so I tightly close my lids.

Tara begins to laugh, followed by Sharla. "Oh. I'm sorry, Blaine. Have we made you uncomfortable? Didn't mean for your ears to fall victim of our little lovefest. Or, maybe it's just karma?" Sharla states as she shrugs and Emmit follows suit before they go into the bathroom and close the door.

I shudder. "Suppose she does have a point, so this should be interesting," I say, turning to Tara whose hands cover her face. "What's wrong?"

Slowly she drags her hands down her face. "She…they heard *us?*"

I nod before I let out a small chuckle. "Who's laughing now, fancy pants?" I pull her petite frame into me as I lift her up and twirl her around, pulling that elusive smile from her and those rose-colored cheeks.

CHAPTER EIGHT

TARA

DINNER WAS NICE AND QUITE INFORMATIVE. I ABSOLUTELY adore the quaint three bedroom house sitting by its lonesome down a dirt road. It still feels awkward calling Margaret 'Ma', but I think I now have a better understanding of why she wants most to call her that. For Margaret, it's more of a term of endearment. Joe was Blaine and Emmit's dad. He and Margaret couldn't have children of their own. Her cousin, Nadine had two small little boys at a young age and their biological father walked out on the three of them. Depressed, Nadine turned to drugs and partying resulting in neglecting her children. Margaret and Joe stepped up and in. Their fight wasn't a hard one. Nadine easily handed her sons over and ran off with a man much older than her.

Our drive home is short, but the silence between us has me on edge. Things are moving fast with us and I get the impression that Blaine wasn't necessarily prepared to revisit those memories with *me* just yet. "Blaine?" I lay my hand across the top of his resting in the front seat of his truck. He glances at me in a show of acknowledgment before facing the open road again. "If there's anything you want to talk about any time, I'm here." He casts his eyes back at me and feigns a grin before resting his elbow on the passenger window while his thumb traces his lower lip. "You didn't judge me, my crazy family, and all the drama that came with them. I'm sorry your mom abandoned you and Emmit."

He yanks his hand from mine. "That druggie bitch was *not* our mom!" I jump, startled at his temper. "Our mom is whose house we were just at. That's the amazing woman that raised us. That other woman just ran off chasing someone like you!" His words leave me puzzled and speechless as he slams his truck into park and gets out, leaving me behind.

He's right. I worded that wrong. I only wanted to let him

know how appreciative I was for him that the same invitation was extended to him. I feel the tears well up as they sting the back of my lids and quickly find freedom, flowing down my cheeks. My phone lights up and I realize it's ringing, but there's no sound. It's Carmen. I click the button on the side to turn my ringer back on.

"Carmen?" I answer through my tears.

"Tara, my sweet girl. I've been calling you for the past few hours. I heard the ramblings around here. Are you okay? You sound like you've been crying," she asks, with heavy concern in her voice.

"I-I thought I was okay. Now, I'm not so sure. I know this sounds crazy, but I thought I'd found something…real. It turns out I might not be able to fly so well after all, Carmen."

"Has somebody hurt you? Other than these assholes around here? I can leave right now and head toward you," she offers.

"No. I'll figure it out. I do miss you so much, though."

A bright light appears behind me walking toward the truck. It's a figure with a flashlight. Must be Blaine.

"Carmen? It's been a long day. Can I call you tomorrow sometime?" I ask, reluctant to hang up with her, but desperately wanting to make things right with Blaine.

The light is approaching quickly.

"Okay, sweet girl. Don't hesitate to call me if you need anything. Love you," she finishes.

"Love you, too."

After ending the call, I hop out of the truck but find myself blinded by the intensity of the light. "Blaine?"

Suddenly I feel something crack against the side of my skull and I become lightheaded as any and all light fades to darkness.

BLAINE

AFTER SEVERAL MINUTES, THE GUILT OF MY ANGER TOWARD Tara overcomes my conscience. I've seen that she's capable of defending herself verbally when pushed too far. But, I suppose she didn't deserve those harsh words that escaped my mouth. My heart aches as I walk outside worried that I'll find her crying yet again. She's had a terrible day. Hell, even with all the money she has, she hasn't had the best life.

As I open the door, the motion detector light is still on. It goes off after two minutes. Rushing to the passenger side of my truck, I notice the door wide open. "Tara?" She's not in here and her car is gone, too. Fuck! "Tara!" I yell out as I pace around the back of the building and see no sign of her. Approaching the front parking lot, I holler at the top of my lungs as loud as possible, "Tara!"

I drop to my knees and feel my heart hammer against my chest. I don't fucking cry, but if she's left, I have nobody to blame but myself and my hurtful words. Retrieving my cell from my back pocket, I call her phone. It begins to ring, and I hear it somewhere behind me. I race back over to where I hear it and find it on the ground under my truck, cracked and nearly shattered. As I look around I notice droplets of blood, so I hang up and call Sheriff Hall. Afterwards, I call my brother and my ma, too.

Everyone arrives at once, but I stop them from driving over any of the blood and direct them to the side of the front parking lot. I've already traced as much of this parking lot as I can, and the drops of blood stop suddenly near the entrance. So, someone plotted and planned this. I will destroy them for this shit!

They all rush to me, but I'm only interested in speaking to Sheriff Hall at the moment. "Tell me what we have here, Blaine." He begins his quest to help me figure out what happened to Tara. He and my dad were great friends and he was always like an uncle to us.

"Look." I point to the droplets of blood with the flashlight from my phone as I walk and show him the trail leading to the truck.

On his radio he dispatches, "All units. We've got a possible kidnapping or…" He stops and looks at me, apologetically and sympathetically. "Could be a possible victim of that bobcat on the loose. Can we get all available units to 'One Knight Stand' along with a search and recovery team?"

"A what?" I grab his arms tightly. "You're kidding me, right? Search and fucking recovery team? No!" He pries my hands free of his arms with help from Emmit. "Sheriff, there's not near enough blood for this to be that fucking bobcat! Someone has fucking taken her and I'm not gonna just stand around here while they get further and further away with my girl!"

"Blaine, honey," my ma says, in an attempt to calm me. She runs her hand soothingly up and down my arm. "Try to calm down for just one second."

"Blaine. I need a description of Tara," Sheriff Hall informs me, and time stands still in that moment as memories of her body, and face play on loop in my mind. Her laugh. That soft angelic giggle. I can almost hear it. "Blaine!"

I snap my eyes up to him. "Um, yeah. Tara Elizabeth

Billings. Five-foot-one. One-hundred-ten pounds. Brunette hair…" My thoughts carry me away again as I speak each one of her traits aloud.

"Good. And her eyes?" he asks, while writing this down.

My heart descends deep into the pit of my stomach when her honey-colored eyes slam into the forefront of my mind. "Unlike anything I've ever seen. The only place I wanna be. Home," I mutter out, my voice cracks and I lower my head in shame and guilt.

"They're a light brown," I hear Emmit tell Sheriff Hall.

I look over to my ma before I shift my gaze to Sharla who's standing idly by holding Jett on her hip. "Keep an eye on Ma, huh? I'm not waiting around here. If Tara somehow shows back up here, call me *immediately!*" Turning to my brother, I ask, "You coming with me? I'm about to go knock on every door in Rose City until I find her if that's what it takes." Emmit nods and we jog to my truck and hop in. "Call Big Boy," I tell my brother as I peel out the parking lot. "Let him know what's going on. He still has her information. That boy seems to know and find things he shouldn't. Tell him I'll pay him well. I just want her back." Fuck! I slam my hands against the leather of my steering wheel.

In an instant my brother's on the phone with Big Boy. From the spying on their conversation while driving, I take it Big Boy already knew from his police scanner. Emmit just answers with the occasional "M-hm's" and "Got it" before he ends the call. "And? Come on, what'd he say?" I switch my bright lights on as we fly down the open road. I have no idea if I'm going in the right direction, but I can't just sit around. What if her family has hired someone to do this? To bring her back home? Whoever has my girl will regret this after I firmly wrap my hands around their neck and watch happily while squeezing the life out of it.

"He's already hacked into something he uses to, well, hack people's shit. I don't know, Blaine. I'm electronically challenged. He heard everything from the police scanner and is running a GPS locator on her vehicle. He said give him a few more minutes and he'll have it," Emmit says, frustrated.

I feel a subtle sigh of relief fill me inside. Please, please let this work. Let her be okay. This is all my fault and I'd never forgive myself if anything were to happen to her. My phone rings, sending a jolt of adrenaline through my body. It's Big Boy.

"Talk to me," I answer.

"Got a location on her car. It's at Gwendolyn Foster's house. I know she frequents the bar, so not sure if you know the address or not…" I cut his words off.

"Thanks Big! I know where that is! Owe you one!"

Ending our phone call, I slam to a near-screeching halt as my tires skid across the pavement before I turn around simultaneously. "Fuck, Blaine!" Emmit hollers out, with his fingers firmly wrapped around the 'bitch bar'. "You're gonna kill us before you get her back!"

"Fucking Gwen, Em! Her car is at Gwen's!" I roar, feeling the rattle of the growl in my throat. "That crazy bitch! Don't you dare say a fucking word right now either about this!" I firmly warn him. He can save any need to express how right he was about Gwen for another time. Now is *not* it.

We turn down the dirt road that Gwen's house is located on and turn my headlights off, only keeping my parking lights on. "What's our plan, bro? We just gonna kick her door in and beat her ass? I mean we can't do that. Gwen's a twisted bitch for this shit, but she's still a woman."

The impulse to snap her fucking neck does cross my mind. Female or not. As we approach, immediately I notice the back of Tara's car nearly hidden behind Gwen's house. "Blaine! Look!" Emmit points to a red truck parked behind Gwen's car in her driveway. "Is that..." I sharply cut him off.

"Fucking Ray! Hand me my nine-millimeter from the glovebox, Em." He reaches in and hands it to me hesitantly.

"Blaine. You're not really gonna kill anybody are you?"

I turn my parking lights off and pull over in between some trees, shrouded by tall brush. "Call Sheriff Hall, Em. Stay here, but I'm getting Tara back."

"You're not going in alone." He grabs the shotgun hidden behind my front cab and cocks it. "Let's go get her."

Crouching down, we walk through the brush as we cautiously approach the house. Ray's a sadistic fuck, so we have to be cautious. If we die, Tara's as good as dead and I won't let that happen. We lean our backs up against the siding of Gwen's house, stopping occasionally as we hear noise from inside. I can hear Ray and Gwen arguing. Looking at Emmit, I place my finger over my lips, ordering him to remain silent. Pointing upward, I notion to him to listen from the window above our heads.

"What exactly do I get out of this besides playing with little miss princess in there?" I hear Ray ask. My veins constrict at the thought of him touching her at all with his grimy hands.

"What do I care? Once I convince Blaine the baby I'm carrying is his, he'll have no choice but to be with me." Gwen replies, and I feel my eyes narrow. That lying, scandalous bitch. She truly is crazy. I wore a rubber every damn time. One-hundred percent foolproof? No. But I know she gets around, too.

"And if he demands a paternity test? Not to mention, my genes are strong. You know this kid's gonna come out looking just like me," Ray's admission clears that right up.

"Blaine's a broke ass, small town bar owner. You really think he's gonna waste money on a paternity test? It doesn't matter. I'll figure it out. Once I'm back in with him and Emmit, I'll slowly begin to plant some of Karen's things around his room. This isn't gonna happen overnight, Ray. Just trust the process. I'll have Sharla doubting Emmit in no time. That's when you can swoop in and be her 'knight.' Not Emmit." I hear Gwen giggle before it turns into a muffled sound combined with some gurgling.

"Don't fuck me over, bitch. I'll come and kill your ass. Pregnant or not," I hear Ray spit out with venom.

There's some sort of struggle inside and I've heard enough. "Ray's always carrying a gun, Em. You know this. I'll kick the door in. I'm not sure what happens after that, but once I lock eyes with him, it's over. He'll draw his weapon and I have to kill him before he kills me," I whisper to my brother.

He nods. "I'm right here. I've got your back. Literally. This is buckshot, right?" he asks in a whisper, and I nod.

I motion forward, and we approach the front door slowly

and quietly with our guns aimed and ready. I look at my brother one last time before I tip my head. Using my entire body and leg strength, I smash the front door in a single kick, nearly removing it from the hinges. My nine is aimed in front of me as I point it in the direction I heard these two sick fucks arguing. Sirens echo around us, getting closer. My eyes make immediate contact with Ray. His eyes grow large and I notice and sense the fear clouding them. He turns quickly toward the back door and runs. I race after him and watch him run on foot like the little bitch he is through the open land behind Gwen's house. "I've got Gwen," Emmit hollers out. I glance over my shoulder to see him holding her in his sight with the shotgun. Her hands are up in the air while she pleads for instant forgiveness. "Sheriff's here and all the deputies. Go find Tara."

"Where is she?" I ask aloud, walking through Gwen's house frantically opening doors. "Where the fuck is she you bitch?" I roar.

"Basement, Blaine!" my brother hollers out.

The last door I open has stairs and I quickly locate the switch to turn the light on and race down the stairs while I holster my gun in the back of my jeans. "Tara! Tara!" She's bound and gagged to a chair in the corner. Her head is hung low and she isn't responding. I tilt her head back quickly and check for a pulse on her neck with shaky hands. "Come on, fancy pants!" That's it! Yes! She has a strong pulse. Her hair is matted with dried blood to the side of her face. Removing the gag from her mouth, I encourage her to speak to me as I untie the rope from her wrists. Her skin and clothing is drenched from sweat. She's not waking up and I need to get her help quickly. Scooping her into my arms, I carry her up the stairs as I shout and holler with determination for someone, anyone, to help her.

One of the deputies meets me at the top of the stairs. "Medics are on the way," he tells me as he notices the frail state my girl's in.

"She's got a strong pulse, but she's not waking up!" I continue past him, making my way outside in time for the paramedics to pull up. I run toward them with her in my arms and watch them jump out, opening the back doors of the ambulance. Climbing in with her, I carefully place her on the gurney inside and watch helplessly as they begin to speak to her and check her vitals while doing numerous things to help her. Powerless, I watch as my future is being decided before my very eyes. They order me to step away to allow them more room to work on her. From my peripheral, I catch a glimpse of Gwen being escorted in handcuffs into a police cruiser.

"How's she doing?" Emmit approaches me from behind,

placing a hand on my shoulder and I momentarily step out of the ambulance, never removing my eyes from Tara.

I feel myself begin to nervously chew on my lower lip as I watch the EMT's try to wake Tara. "I-I..." my stifled words get lodged in my throat as I feel my eyes begin to water and I force them back down.

"We're going now. She needs to see a trauma doctor. We're taking her to RCMC. Sir, are you coming?" the female medic asks me.

I slyly pull my gun from the back of my jeans and pass it behind me to Emmit before I toss him my keys. "You know where we'll be," I tell him before I load up in the back of the ambulance with my girl. My eyes trail up her legs to her arm that has an IV now placed in it as they give her fluids. An oxygen mask covers her nose and mouth and she's strapped firmly to the gurney, still not awake. What have these monsters done? I wanna cry. I wanna scream. I wanna beat the shit out of anything in this moment. I just wanna feel anything other than...this. Taking her hand into mine, I silently pray that wherever her subconscious is in this moment that she can feel me. Hoping she can hear my heart as it begs with every beat for her to come back to me. I glance out the back window of the ambulance and notice they caught Ray and he, too, is being escorted to a police cruiser. Lucky fucker. Whatever punishment he's given will be far less than what he deserves.

———

ONCE WE ARRIVED, THE TRAUMA TEAM ASKED ME SEVERAL questions most of which I had no clue of how to answer before kicking me out into the waiting area. Sheriff Hall showed up right behind us, questioning me. We decided that I would come down to the station and give my official statement after I knew Tara was gonna be okay. The near-vacant waiting area of this cold, sterile environment quickly fills with my friends and family.

"How is she?" Ma asks with tear-stained cheeks, and I wrap my arms around her.

"She's gonna be okay, Ma," I reply, hoping to convince someone because that hope is all I have in this moment to hang onto.

"Why aren't they letting you back there?"

I shrug. "I'm not family? Not by their policy standards, anyway."

"Like hell!" My ma walks over to the nurse's desk and I follow behind her after receiving quick hugs from everyone. "Excuse me?" The young, blonde nurse looks up. "Who's Tara Billings' doctor?"

"Are you family?" the nurse asks, with a hint of snark in her tone.

"You're damn right I am. I'm her ma and I demand to speak with her doctor now." She slams her purse up on the desk.

"I'll go check, ma'am," the nurse says, as she stands and walks away.

"Little blonde bimbo. No offense, Sharla," my ma says, turning around.

"None taken, Ma. My fellow blondes are giving us all a bad reputation today," Sharla responds before the nurse comes back with a grin showcased on her face.

"Doctor Wells will be out here shortly to update you all," she informs us.

Ma looks at me. "James Wells. I sort of figured. That's why I asked. If not, I was gonna call him. We graduated the same year. Last time I saw him was years ago at mine and your father's high school reunion." She cups my face. "Tara's in good hands, honey."

"Margaret?" the tall grey-haired man inquires approaching my ma. "Now, we both know that's not your daughter in there. But, she must be someone important to have you out here stirring up the nurse," he says in a teasing manner. I feel myself growing more pissed by the second.

"Yes, she is someone important. She's my girlfriend and I'm growing more agitated by the second not knowing what's going on back there. So, if the two of you could catch up over coffee later, that'd be great. For now, I need to know what the hell is going on," I say, raising my tone, alerting him to my anger and building frustration.

Everyone crowds around, casting inquisitive eyes on the doctor. "She's dehydrated, so we're giving her fluids. She's just been taken to CT to have a scan done. It appears she's had some sort of blunt trauma to her head. Her vitals otherwise are nice and stable. Now, boyfriend, do you have a name?"

"Blaine Knight. Her son." I nod my head toward my ma. "When can I see her?"

"If you want to come back to her room now, she shouldn't be too much longer. Now, it will take a few minutes until we have the results from her scans, but I've put an obvious rush on it," he answers me, and I waste no time making my way to those double doors standing in my way.

"Let's go, doc. I wanna be there if she's awake. Or at least when she wakes."

He turns to face me, but briefly turns back to my ma. "Can't blame a man in love."

Love? Impossible. Sure, she means a lot to me, but we barely know one another. Am I acting like a man in love? Do other's see something that I don't? Fuck. Am I in love? No, it's too early to declare this as love. Right?

CHAPTER NINE

BLAINE

Doctor Wells escorts me to Tara's room and I race through the door in hopes that her beautiful face will be on the other side to greet me. It's not. There's a large empty spot in the middle of the room where her bed must go. It's quite dark in here aside from the few machines that I have no clue what they are or used for.

"Your ma's a friend of mine," Doctor Wells tells me.

Letting out a heavy sigh, I reply, "So I hear. High school. Look." I rub my hands down my face. "Can we just cut the shit, please? I'm asking nicely. Forget all the medical terminology. Explain this to me in layman's terms, huh?"

"Well, Blaine, her vitals are all normal and stable. She's breathing entirely on her own. Her labs, or bloodwork, all look normal. I can't say with certainty until we have the CT scan results back. I've been doing this a lot of years and the last thing I want to do is give a loved one false hope. But, off the record, it's my opinion that she probably has a concussion due to the blow to her head. Which did require several stitches, but nothing drastic. Combine that with her being dehydrated, and that's exactly what this looks like it could be. Meaning, I think she will regain consciousness once her body is hydrated and rested…off the record," he emphasizes. "Again, I should know more soon."

"Will she suffer from memory loss?"

"Far too early to tell. But I don't think so. Off the record again, of course," he answers.

Folding my arms across my chest, I nervously chew on my bottom lip as I nod. It feels as though my heart leaps into my throat with optimism, though. Of course, there's always that chance, like he just said. Refusing to let the negative thoughts invade and take up residence in my head, I replace them with faith. Pure, and completely full of hope. It's all I have, and she's got to be okay, so I can apologize for the rest of my living days for lashing out on her and leaving her alone.

Two nurses appear with Tara, still unconscious in that bed. Looking at her in this condition wrecks my soul. I race to be at her side and take her tiny, fragile hand in mine. "Hey, fancy pants. I'm here." I bring her hand to my lips and press them firmly against her soft skin, closing my eyes. "I don't know if you can hear me right now or not, but it's time to wake up, okay? They say it's probably a mild concussion. You're safe now. I'm never leaving your side again. I just need you to give me one more chance to prove that. This…this thing between us…I'm not sure yet what it is exactly, but I can tell that I've never in my life felt this way about anyone else. Ever. Sounds fucking corny, I know. We've known each other only a few days, but I can't quit you. I won't, Tara. Please?" I squeeze her hand a little firmer. "I need for you to open those gorgeous eyes that engulf me, leaving me paralyzed and at their mercy."

"W-who are you?" Tara's stammers out in a raspy, dry voice. "Do I know you?"

My eyes shoot wide open and find hers. Relief washes over me as I exhale, but her words gut me. It's as if someone has reached inside my chest and completely ripped my heart out and I physically feel my body as it slumps over in the chair. "Tara it's me, Blaine." I swallow hard, praying she remembers me. Us. Anything about us and these past few days.

Doctor Wells walks back in. "Oh, our lovely patient is now awake. I'm Doctor Wells and I need to check your pupils." He takes a miniature flashlight and shines it in each of her eyes. "Perfect. Do you know your name?"

"Of course. I'm Tara Billings," she answers, proudly.

"Tara, do you know where you are?" he asks her, and I snap my eyes from him back to her, desperate for each answer to jog her memory.

"Judging by the fact that you're a doctor and I'm hooked up to a ton of equipment with an IV in my arm…my guess is a hospital," she replies before a grin curls up on her lips. "My head." She reaches for it as she winces out. "Damn it hurts." She shifts her gaze to me. Her eyes harbor a hint of something mischievous. "That bitch named Gwen hit me over the back of the head with a heavy ass flashlight. And don't even get me started with that nasty waste of human space named Ray. Blaine Michael Knight, I hope you took care of him. Leaving me all alone in your truck with nothing but darkness."

"Yes, you've got a mild concussion all things considered. A few stitches. But they're on the scalp. Should heal up nicely and nobody will ever be the wiser," Doctor Wells informs her.

She remembers me. She remembers us. My heartrate picks up in pace as I feel an enormous smile cross my face. "So, you were just faking? You remembered me the entire time?"

"Yes." She grins before she giggles that harmonious tune I prayed to hear once more. "Listen, buddy. You got played for all of one minute. I was knocked out and kidnapped. Hell, I've got a concussion and stitches to top it off. I'd say in comparison, you got off easy. Plus, how could I stop you? You were all but promising yourself to me forever."

I grin before a chuckle breaks free and I lean up, kissing her forehead. "I have no idea what you speak of. Must be the concussion." She bats at my arm but winces out in pain. "Easy there, fancy pants. I take it back. I just need you to rest. And for the record, I meant everything I said. And absolutely none of what I said earlier before all hell broke loose."

Her eyes blink slowly, as she begins to fall back asleep. I wanna beg her to stay with me longer, but I know her body is exhausted and needs rest. "I know. If that's your apology, I forgive you," she finishes before she closes her eyes one final time.

Gently and carefully, I push a strand of hair away from her face. "Rest. Just remember to come back to me."

TARA

My eyes invite a throbbing that rivals the worst hangover I've ever had. Yep, I'm still in the hospital. This wasn't a terrible nightmare, but the silver lining is that everything that Blaine said while he thought I was still unconscious was real. As I try to focus my hazy vision, I feel Blaine's hand on top of mine. He's asleep in a chair, but his head lays on the side of the bed next to me. This man. My heart. How is this possible? I've never simply looked at someone and felt my entire body explode inside with such a warmth. This is what fairytales and movies are made of, not real life. It seems impossible that I could love or be in love with him after such a short period of time. We still know next to nothing about one another. Yet, I can't deny that this feels different than anything I ever felt for Preston. This goes much deeper. Is this what it really feels like to love someone? I knew I cared deeply for Blaine but looking at him vigil at my bedside stirs up something deep within me that I've never felt before. He looks so peaceful right now it would just be downright sinful to wake him. I know I'm the one in the hospital bed, but this looks like it's taken far worse of a toll on him than me.

An elderly woman comes in wearing navy blue scrubs and

a smile much too chipper for me at the moment. "Morning. How are you feeling?" she asks.

I place a finger from my free hand over my lips and shush her while I shift my gaze to Blaine. "I feel like I was hit over the head with a flashlight," I whisper at her.

"And fancy pants is awake," I hear Blaine's raspy voice and turn to him. "I'm learning she can be a real smartass at times. Don't let her fool ya. She's a sweet one, sure. But, when provoked, those claws and fangs make an appearance." I narrow my eyes at him and feel my lips thin.

"I resent that, actually." I yank my hand from his and quickly learn how sore I really am.

"Whoa, Tara. You've just been through a traumatic event. Both mentally and physically. So feisty. Be easy on yourself," he expresses, pressing his lips to my forehead as he stands.

The nurse takes my vitals before she begins questioning my medical history. "Any allergies to medications? Major surgeries?"

"Nope."

"Any current medications you take daily such as birth control?" she asks, writing my answers down in her chart.

"Yes." I nod. "I take the pill." Dragging my eyes to Blaine,

I ask, "My purse? Have you seen it? I haven't taken it today." Judging by his expression, I get the impression he doesn't have a clue. "It's fine. If I have to I can replace all of my belongings."

"It was in the truck…I think," he finally answers. "Everything happened so fast, but I think I remember seeing it in the seat."

"If you need a new prescription, we can have Doctor Wells write you a new one?" the nurse offers.

"That would be great, thanks," I tell her. "Any idea how long I'll be in here?"

"Doctor Wells has signed off on your release. All I have to do now is get him to write your script, and you can be on your way." She stops writing and glances up, offering me a smile.

So many things to do still and each time another task fills my head, I feel consumed by a sense of being overwhelmed. I need new clothes still. Now I might need to call all of my credit card companies and banks and inform them my information might've been breached. Suddenly it dawns on me that I haven't seen my parents. Fear and anxiety slither their advances into my thoughts. I don't want any of them here.

"Blaine!" I jolt straight up in the bed causing a sudden

rush to my head, leaving me wincing and clutching the back of my hair.

In seconds he's kneeling at my side. "What's wrong? What is it, Tara?" He places his hand lovingly on my arm.

"Do my parents know? Please say nobody's called them," I beg.

He begins to rub his hand softly up and down my forearm. "No, fancy pants. It was a judgement call, and I made it."

I place my hands on the sides of his face and pull him closer to me, so I can place a kiss on his forehead. The feel of my lips on his flesh holds me captive longer than it should. "Thank you," I whisper across his skin.

His eyes slowly raise to meet mine and no words are needed as we stare at one another. His eyes convey a language and emotion all their own, and it's one I understand. I nod before I feel a grin tug upward on my face.

"Now, let's get this IV out of you and I'll go over all of your discharge instructions along with your prescription," the nurse interrupts. I'm unsure if she left momentarily or has been here this entire time, but it doesn't matter. Logic tells me that she had to have left to get me a signed prescription, but I was too wrapped up in the moment I was sharing with Blaine to notice or care.

BLAINE

ONCE WE ARRIVE BACK AT THE BAR, I'M PLEASED TO SEE her car parked safely here once again. My entire family is waiting to greet Tara the second we enter. It seems like everyone is rushing in on her at once, and I can feel myself becoming more aggravated by the second. Don't get me wrong, I'm glad they all care so much for her and her well-being, but she's tired and still sore. I watch for a fleeting moment as she warmly returns their sincere embraces. I watch the subtle winces and expressions that cross her face. She's genuinely happy for their care and concern and would let them yap her ear off for days if I allowed. She naturally puts others before herself even if it's to her own detriment. But I on the other hand, won't allow her to self-martyr for their benefit. She's already got a long road ahead of her today alone. I haven't told her yet, but Sheriff Hall will be here later to take her official state-ment. He wanted to do it late last night after she'd already fallen back asleep. I pleaded for him to wait and at least allow her to be somewhere more comforting than the cold, and uninviting energy of that hospital that's surrounded by nothing but sickness and death.

"Okay, folks." I step in and between my family. "I need to get her upstairs and back to resting."

Murmurs of disapproval echo accompanied by understanding. "Hey, Sharla? You wouldn't happen to know what happened to my purse would you?" Tara turns and asks her.

Shit. Her purse. I almost forgot. I cast my gaze toward Sharla who shifts her eyes from Tara to me before she nods. "Yes. Sheriff Hall currently has it. Said he'd bring it by later when he stopped by to get your statement," Sharla turns her eyes back to Tara as she answers her.

Tara swiftly turns to me and I know immediately I probably should've discussed that with her on our way back. "I'm gonna call him once you've had some more rest and get some proper food in you."

I watch her gulp and it's audible, too. I notice the darkness of fear creeping into her eyes before she lowers them to the floor. "I-I don't know if I'm ready, Blaine. I mean…"

I sharply cut her words off. "You don't have to say anything right now. Let's just take this one minute at a time, huh?" She nods, still staring down. Now is the time I need to stay calm for her sake, but my blood feels like it's turning to lava with each pump of my heart, melting me from the inside out. How dare those two wastes of human space think it was okay to harm someone else for their own selfish reasons. Especially my fancy pants. Staring at her in this moment has me more certain than ever that she was sent to me, *for* me. She's changed me dramatically in such a short period of time, and I will protect her at all costs. From this moment forward, my need to both love and protect her is primal and animalistic. I scoop her off her feet, and as if she was instinctively expecting it, she wraps her arms around my neck and buries her head into my chest. "I'm taking her upstairs. Any and everyone from this moment on will go through me first before even speaking to her until I am sure she feels safe and secure again. Don't take offense from my words. It's nothing personal. I love you all and you know it. But I love this woman more than I care about anyone's feelings. Even my own." They look at me stunned in silence. "You feel strong enough to stand in the shower?" I feel her nod, gesturing she can. "Let's get you cleaned up. I'll get you something comfy of mine to wear," I whisper into her hair and she nods again. Yeah, I said it earlier. I fucking love her. Nobody has ever made me feel things the way she does. So, if this isn't what love is, then I guess I'll never know. But I know that I never want to be without her and my heart wants to explode inside my chest at the very thought of her. Or when her name crosses my mind or is spoken.

CHAPTER TEN

TARA

I'VE NEVER HAD A MAN CARE FOR ME THE WAY THAT Blaine has. He climbed in the shower behind me and washed my body with a delicacy I've never known. The way he gently traced my body like I was expensive irreplaceable fine china. Not a single word was spoken between us. It was one of the most sensual experiences of my life. All I kept thinking of was how he'd just declared his love for me. It didn't go unnoticed and it took me by surprise.

Blaine gently lays me down on his bed and begins to position pillows around me before he literally tucks blankets around me. I lay here in near disbelief with touches of confusion. I don't know if this is a normal reaction from a man when he loves a woman…or if this is just, well, too much.

"Blaine!" I shout, the echo of my own voice has my head ringing again instantly. His eyes quickly meet mine. "I'm fine, please." I push the covers back over my body and watch as his demeanor shifts. He glares at me as if I've upset him. "Just stop. And don't look at me like that. Everything you're doing for me I am more than grateful for, but all it's doing is reminding me of, well, how fragile and weak I really am."

He steps toward me and begins to try to cover me once again. "Tara, you need rest."

"No!" I stand abruptly and am again reminded of the nagging ache in my head. I grab my jeans and slide them up my legs, leaving his t-shirt on before slipping into my shoes.

"Tara?" his voice pleads to me. I know he senses that I've reached my limit of frustration and confusion and I need to retreat.

I look over at him hesitantly as tears sting the back of my lids. "Blaine, I love you too. Fuck. At least I think I do. I mean is it really possible to love or fall for someone so deeply in such a short period of time? In a few short days I've experienced things, emotions that I never thought were possible. I've also been kidnapped by two psychotic and twisted individuals for their own personal gain…so they could either have you or someone you're close to. Is love supposed to be like this? Both times now in my life I thought I loved someone, nothing but sorrow and trauma surrounded it. If loving you, or you loving me means that I will never be safe from all of the past notches on your bedpost…then I need to rethink this."

"That's not fair, Tara. You're hitting below the belt now. What happened to you was out of my control," he says through a shaky, cracked voice as his eyes begin to water.

I feel my heart cry out inside because I the last thing I ever want to do is hurt this man. Ever. He told me how hard it was for him to admit the way he was beginning to feel for me. And how he wasn't just handing his heart over to anyone. But, can I live like this? If loving him is going to keep me in constant danger, is it worth it? Am I just being selfish right now? Is this the concussion talking? The only way to know is to put some space between us, at least for now. "I need some time." Tears fall simultaneously down my cheeks when the words leave my lips. "Tell Sheriff Hall to contact me and he and I can set something up. I guess I can make arrangements to get my purse from him, too. I'm so fucking sorry," I admit. "I can only hope you'll understand my need for some time to myself right now." I place a soft kiss on his cheek and walk past him, grabbing my car keys off his dresser.

"I'm begging you, Tara. Don't do this, please?" I can feel his heart shatter in his tone and it feels like my own soul is being ripped form my body.

"I don't expect for you to wait for me Blaine. I won't ask that of you. But I am asking for some time," I finish saying, my back toward his as I don't wait for any further reply from him before I fly down the stairs. Passing everyone, I never stop to answer any of their questions. I've got to get out of here before someone tries to stop me.

BLAINE
Three Months Later

IT'S BEEN MONTHS SINCE I'VE PHYSICALLY SEEN TARA, BUT each day has felt like a year. At first, I tried to contact her, but she refused to speak to me. She's kept in contact with Sharla, but all I get from Sharla is crumbs where Tara's concerned. About a month ago she started calling again, but every time I answer, she never spoke a word and eventually just hung up. I feel lost, as if I'm motioning through life on autopilot. My bedroom became a prison of memories I shared with her. So, after two weeks of that shit, I had myself a house built. Nothing fancy at all. A small two bedroom cabin on several acres of land. Emmit has moved in with Sharla, so the bar is just that now. I've debated handing my half of ownership over to my brother, but honestly, work is the only thing that keeps my mind off the one fucking thing I've ever truly loved and lost.

"You gonna go?" Emmit asks me before taking a sip of his coffee. He and Sharla come by regularly to check on me and keep me from permanently slipping into the darkness threatening to devour my consciousness.

"To Gwen and Ray's sentencing? Is that even a legitimate question?" I trace the rim of my coffee mug with my finger. "Watching those two get a fraction of what I feel they deserve it something I wouldn't miss. You already know this, brother."

"She's undecided, ya know?" Sharla says, immediately catching my attention. "They pled guilty. So, she can go and give a victim impact statement, but I honestly don't think she is."

The thought of seeing her again has my heart feeling like it's about to leap from my chest. Well, that's before the deep sadness of Sharla's last sentence hits me. I've wanted to throw the towel in on any possible chance we might have on many occasions, but my heart won't let me. I don't know if it ever will and it's not something I can explain to anyone to the point of understanding. Fuck fairytales and love stories. That shit's for the movies. Or so I thought. Love at first sight? Nah. I never believed in that because I honestly never believed in love. Until Tara. One look in those entrancing eyes of hers and it was as if I was given a peek into heaven. She was so pure, innocent, and well, naïve. It frustrated me instantly because I felt her presence stir up something unimaginable inside of me. I had a sense of just knowing that this one petite woman would have a major impact on my life forever. Although I didn't realize it at the time, in that moment, she stole a piece of my heart and will own it forever. Maybe this is grief, or a stage of it? I'm not ready to accept that she will never come back to me even though my family are forever advising me to move on. They just can't understand it's not as simple as that, but God I wish it were. What would I be moving on from exactly when I know that I will forever compare any other woman and potential connection to the one I shared with Tara. It was brief, fleeting, but so intense that nothing or nobody will ever compare.

"How you holding up?" I glance up, asking Sharla. "I know it can't be easy accepting what Jett's father did and that he's looking at up to ten years in prison considering his priors."

She pours creamer into her coffee and looks up at me. "Honestly? Jett's better off without him. I used to convince myself that no matter how horrible Ray was to me, that I couldn't just take Jett from him. Now? This has forced me to face the truth." She rubs Emmit's back. "Em is a much better role model for Jett and the man we both need in our lives." After an exchange of googly eyes, they lean in and kiss.

I feel nauseous. Don't get me wrong, I'm glad they found happiness and in one another, but it only serves to remind me of what's missing from my own life. "Yeah. You're one-hundred percent right about that." I stand and walk toward my kitchen sink to wash out my mug. "I'm gonna go shower. Oh, has anyone called or applied for the new waitress position yet before I forget to ask later? I haven't received any calls."

They both look at me and shake their heads. "Finally got you to agree and now we can't even fucking pay to get some help in there. We need it bad too, Blaine. With the new chain of stores and subdivision being built, business is picking up."

I nod. "Yeah. I know. Y'all gonna stay or are you all going to Ma's?"

"We're gonna head over early," Emmit stands, replying to me as he stretches.

"I'll see ya both later. I've got a few invoices to pay and another order to place before I head over."

"See ya later, Blaine," I hear Sharla tell me after I walk away toward my bedroom.

TARA

Leaving Blaine might not have been the right thing to do at the time, but it was the right thing for me. I hired a moving crew to go and personally retrieve all of my belongings at my penthouse and leased a quaint little house about an hour from my parents and sister. After everything that happened, I was considered the town pariah. Typical. Honestly, I expected nothing less, so my parents disowning me was no shocker either. My sister on the other hand made several attempts to contact me and wanted reconciliation. Silly little twit that she is. She didn't truly want a fresh start or new relationship with me. Hell, she wasn't sorry even though she said it multiple times on messages. The bitch was only sorry she got caught as her recent actions have proven. I'll admit that the engagement announcement of my sister and Preston momentarily shook the ground beneath me, but I quickly found my footing.

My therapist has continually helped me find ways to manage my anger, betrayal, resentment, and fear. Not just from the situation with Preston and then what happened to me with Blaine. No. She helped me realize that years of conditioning and lack of self-worth were all combinations of situations I had been subject to. I've taken back my life and have a sense of empowerment. I'm only a victim of these things if I allow them to define me. I choose not to. Which is exactly why I have zero desire to give a victim impact statement at Gwen and Ray's sentencing hearing. Sure, I hope they get the punishment they deserve so they never have the chance to harm another individual. However, I feel no need to stand before them and give them any more power over me. They know what they did and that they're guilty, but I refuse to stand before them and let them watch me tell the tale of how deeply they changed my life that night. I think as sick and twisted as they are that would only feed into their sickness.

Carmen left my parents and has come to stay with me. When lines were seemingly drawn in the sand, she chose to stand by my side and has been one of my rocks through this entire ordeal. Sharla has been the other. I've cut off every one of my old friends. Or, they began to slowly cut me out, so I made the decision easier for all of us and let them go.

I asked Sharla not to tell Blaine anything too specific about me and what I was doing. In turn, she gave me the same treatment I'd asked her to give Blaine concerning me. I suppose that was fair enough. I *never* wanted to hurt him, ever. I genuinely felt something special between us and I still do. From the beginning, the way we met almost seemed fated or serendipitous. It all began with me having an utter meltdown and running from one situation, to me leaving him in a similar fashion. Almost as if in a few short days whatever foundation we were building on came full circle and crumbled. I may never be forgiven by him for the abrupt way I ended things, but I am healed and better now. So, even though I haven't quite figured out how yet, I do plan on making an attempt to see him. I have both mentally and emotionally prepared myself for his rejection.

"My sweet girl. What are you daydreaming about now?" Carmen interrupts my thoughts as I look out into the beautiful back yard of my little home that's blanketed by a small field of Dahlias. She hands me a cup of fresh-brewed coffee and sits down next to me on the plush window seat. "Honey, I know you do love this man. And I can promise you this. If it was meant to be, he will understand your need to go heal and find your way. Because in the end he will realize it brought you back to him." She places her hand on my knee. "Love is a funny thing, ya know?" She giggles under her breath. "It catches us off-guard and forces us to face our insecurities and vulnerabilities." I cast my gaze to her. I feel as though she's speaking from personal experience, but I've never once heard her speak of being married. I've always wondered but simply figured she chose us over herself. I stare as I listen intently. "I've never told you this, but I loved once. His name was Sergio." She removes her eyes from the window and looks at me. "Sexy name, huh?" I nod as it is indeed a unique name that screams of intensity. "You were three. I was given a paid vacation for two weeks and your mother had to basically pry us from one another. I honestly didn't want to leave you, but your parents insisted. Anyway, about a week into my vacation I walked to the vegetable market downtown. That's where I met Sergio." I watch her eyes light up and a smile form on her face. She turns back to the flowers outside. "He ran a tomato stand. Our eyes locked and I was a goner. It was as if time stood still and everything around us just ceased to exist. Once I composed myself and bought my tomatoes, I walked away while my soul screamed for me to go back and talk with him. My bag ripped open after about, oh, I'd say five steps. He rushed to my side and not only did he replace my now ruined tomatoes, he double bagged the next batch." She giggles again. God I always loved hearing her sing to me and tell me stories. But I've never heard this one. "The rest of the walk home I mentally chastised myself for being a coward and not getting his phone number. Once I began unpacking the vegetables, I found a little note inside the bag with his name and telephone number. I paced the floor for hours and got little to no sleep that night. I thought of all the repercussions if I were to get involved in a relationship. What if I fell madly in love and we decided to move?" She casts her eyes back to me and I notice a pool of water in them. I reach out and place my hand on hers. Dear God, what happened? Did she choose me over this possible love she had? Please let the answer to that be no. "I called the next evening. We talked for hours and it was as if we'd known each other our entire lives. The next evening he took me out for dinner. Honey we spent four glorious days and nights together, and I can say with an honest heart that I *loved* that man. A week after I'd went back to work and to you, his brother called to tell me that he'd been hit by a car walking to the market for work and didn't survive." I watch the crystal clear droplets fall from her lids and onto her jeans. She takes both of my hands into hers and squeezes them tightly. "I never thought for a single second that you were crazy and that it was impossible for two people to fall in love so suddenly. You needed to heal, honey. From all of it. You might not have known it at the time and maybe he didn't either or still doesn't. But, my darling girl, it's time. Let me ask you this. What did it feel like when you looked into his eyes?"

Her question catches me by surprise. My heart is feels like it's literally bleeding for her right now and she's wanting to know about me? I let out a heavy sigh because discussing me, or me and Blaine right now just feels downright selfish.

"Tara Elizabeth." My eyes slowly rise upward and stare back at her. "Answer my question."

"Safe. Peaceful. Like I'd known him for my entire life." Frustrated by my own answers, I stand with my back toward her, placing my hands upon my hips. Turning back to face her, I declare, "It felt like where I belonged. There, are you happy?"

She stands with a stern look on her face before she begins to point her finger toward me and says, "Am I happy? Tara this isn't about me, sweetie. This is about you. Are you happy? Sounds to me like Blaine is where you find happiness. Why would you deny yourself that?" She walks up to me and places her hands on my shoulders. "I've watched you for months now. I've listened to you and the love, longing, passion, and ache in your voice when you speak of him. I told you my experience for a reason. This, whatever it is, only comes around once. Or at least that's my experience. Once it finds you, it steals a part of your heart and soul that you'll never be able to give to another. Now, grab that bull by the horns and don't you waste another minute. Stop sitting here staring out this window wanting and wishing. Go claim your love. Because tomorrow is not ever promised."

"Carmen, I..." my words get lodged in my throat. My heart is crushed for her and the love she had...and lost.

"Stop thinking so much, Tara. You're trying to use logic for something that only makes sense to the heart. Your mind can't compute nor compete with your heart, although it tricks us into believing so. I didn't tell you my experience, so I could watch you stand around here and feel sad for me. At the end of it all, I wouldn't trade those four days for a lifetime with someone else. No, Tara. Love, true love is always forgiving. It's about loving unconditionally. Through the good and the bad. Are you going to continue to stand here and waste your days away daydreaming, or go find out?" She grabs my purse and shoves it into my arms. "Call or text me once you've made it there safely." She pulls me into her arms and kisses my cheek. "Now go on. Go fly."

BLAINE

AFTER DINNER, I HEAD UP TO THE BAR TO RETRIEVE AN order that was delayed a day due to some heavy storms on the east coast. Emmit offered to help, but I declined. They needed to get Jett home and tucked into bed and I know that Em really enjoys doing that as a family with Sharla.

I'm so happy they found their happiness, but at the same time it always reminds me of what that would've and could've been like with Tara.

I pour myself a drink and slam it back along with my loathing and self-pity, but it does no good. At this point I can't help but find this shit fucking comical. One day I'm strolling merrily along through life having meaningless sex with whatever woman I choose, and all seemed perfect in my world…or so I led myself to believe. A state championship, a storm, a flat tire later and my world was turned upside down. She brought me to life the moment our eyes connected, and I knew somehow life would never be the same. Maybe not consciously at the time, but it was always underlying, and that became abundantly clear after she walked out. Tara has set and raised the bar so damn high that the only thing I fuck is my damn self. And even when I do that it involves her and the memories I share with her.

"Fuck!" I launch the glass across the bar and it shatters against the wall.

I notice an opened pack of smokes behind the bar probably belonging to Emmit or Sharla. Reaching for one, I place it between my lips and light a match when a knock on the door interrupts me. I remove the cigarette and shake the match until the flame is gone, placing it in a nearby ashtray. Placing my hand behind my back and on my gun, I cautiously approach the door. It's late and dark outside. With Ray and Gwen's sentencing date approaching, I can't be too cautious. Anyone that should be here at this hour has a fucking key. The knock is louder and firmer the second time.

"Bar's closed!" I say sternly, warning the person on the other side. I patiently wait for a few seconds and get no response. "I don't think you realize who you're fucking with here," I pop off again, ready to take any action necessary.

"Yeah? Well, the sign outside says you're hiring, and I saw your truck." Electricity courses through my body bringing every limb and nerve to life once I hear her voice. I rub my eyes and swallow thickly. "It's kind of chilly outside. You going to leave me out here?"

My heart rate increases and the blood running through my veins feels like I'm gonna spontaneously combust at any moment. This is it. This is what I've wished for. I whip open the door and there she is. There she stands, shyly gazing into my eyes from under her lashes.

"Can I come in? I mean, I understand if you don't want me to," she explains through a shaky voice.

What the fuck do I do? I'm not a religious man, but right now I'm begging God for an answer. Every part of me wants to reach out and grab her up and into my arms, never to let go again. But I don't wanna rush her or scare her off.

"I am so fucking sorry. This is wrong of me. I can't just walk out of your life suddenly and then show up unannounced like this." She turns to walk away, and I reach out and grab her, risking it all with this one motion.

She swings back around, her eyes searching mine begging for forgiveness. I nod. "Come in." The moment the words leave my lips, I watch a lone tear slide down her cheek and I desperately want to wipe it away.

She studies the bar briefly as she rubs her arms in an attempt to warm herself. Again, I fight my inner self and the driving need to pull her body into mine. "I've got an extra coat in the back I can get for you. I think Emmit might have one he and Sharla keep here. If you want?"

She wipes her cheek and I watch a subtle grin emerge on her face. "I'll be fine. Thank you, though. You look good, Blaine." Watching my name leave her lips nearly has me gasping for air. I've wanted and yearned for the day I could see and hear her again. "Although a job here would be nice, that's not the real reason I came here." Her head falls before she slowly raises it back up, leaving me in utter suspense. "I came here to apologize." Oh fuck. Here it goes. She's come to tie up loose ends, so she can move forward with her life. It's like one of those fucking twelve step programs or some shit. "I don't know if you can ever forgive me for walking out the way that I did, but Blaine, in that moment I had to. I needed to clear my head. To wrap my head around everything that had transpired between us, me, and my family in those few days." She tucks a strand of her hair behind her ear. "In my journey of healing and finding myself and what I value most…I found that I value myself most and my happiness." I wanna scream at her to spit it out. Just tell me that she's on some soul mission and wrapping up our brief past. "In doing that, I realized that as much as I love myself, that Blaine, I do love you. And if you're willing, I'd like a clean slate. A fresh start with you. A nice clean slate. That is of course if you still feel that way about me, and I understand completely if you don't…"

The last of her words barely leave her lips before I grab her and smash my mouth to hers, stealing the breath from her lungs. I'm greedy and I want her, all of her. She reciprocates by swiping her tongue along the entrance to my mouth and I allow her entrance. Our kiss is rough and passionate as our tongues battle for their right to own one another. I want to make up for lost time. Honestly, in this moment, I could be right here with her and never move.

"So, you forgive me? You understand and don't hate me?" she asks, pulling away.

I cup her soft, beautiful face as my heart pounds inside my

chest. "Fancy pants, I forgave you the minute you walked away. I didn't like it because I'm selfish with you. But after some thinking, and reasoning explained by others, I got it. I realized that in being selfish with you, I wasn't allowing you to do whatever it was you needed to do for yourself. No, I could never in this lifetime or any other hate you. Because I love you more than I have ever loved anyone or anything. I've wished for this moment every single day since you left. I love you, Tara Elizabeth Billings." I lean down and gently press my lips to her forehead.

She closes her eyes and smiles at my touch. "So, Sharla did accidentally let it slip that you'd moved out. I honestly didn't figure you'd be here, but I took a chance."

I feel the giddy grin emerge across my face. "I'm glad you did. So fucking glad." I firmly pull her into my body and rest my chin on her head as she wraps her arms tightly around my waist.

"We going to catch up here, or at your place?" she asks, against my chest.

I couldn't rid my face of the grin I feel plastered on it even if I tried right now. "You wanna go to my place?"

I feel her nod, indicating she does. "I'm curious to see it and...reconnect."

Deeply I exhale accompanied by a low unexpected growl

in my throat. We're moving fast, and I'm more than okay with that, but I know I'm gonna want to dive inside her pussy once we're there and show her just how much I've missed her presence. "Okay," I mutter. "But, we're taking my truck. We're doing this together."

She pulls her head back and looks up at me. "Blaine Knight. You wouldn't be trying to make sure I don't somehow get away again would you?" she teases, with a smile on her face.

Without hesitation, I answer, "You're damn right. I just got you back. Don't even worry about your car. I'll buy you ten more God forbid something happen to that one. You're riding with me, fancy pants."

Her eyes grow wide with wonder. "Ten, huh? Not that it matters, but that car is over one-hundred grand. You got some money stashed you never tell anyone about?" she says jokingly, but doesn't understand just how much truth there is behind her question.

"I said what I said, and I meant it," I reply seriously. "Now, let's go." I lower my hand, tracing it down her arm until our fingers meet and intertwine.

CHAPTER ELEVEN

TARA

During the drive to Blaine's new house, he pulled me close and kept his arm around me. The only light illuminating his house as we pull up the long driveway is provided by the beauty of the moon. I feel my eyes grow wide as I mentally note the mirroring image to my own home. I mean sure, they're in different places, but it's quaint, subtle, yet cozy-looking.

I slide out behind him and he reaches out, taking my hand in his before twirling me around until my back is against his chest. His arms snake around my waist and he leans into my ear and whispers, "What do you think? I know it's not the biggest or fanciest, but for some reason when I designed it, I had you in mind." I feel him kiss the back of my hair.

My heart swells at his words and I clutch my chest. "It's utterly perfect, beautiful, and well, it suits you."

"My thoughts exactly," he replies. "Now, let's get you inside." He rubs my arms as I begin to shudder from the cool night breeze.

Once inside, he walks me through each room. Although they're all amazing, his walls are bare, and the interior is mostly empty. Aside from the essentials needed for daily living. Down to the layout of his house and everything, ours are so similar it's nearly surreal. "Blaine?" I turn to him and notice I have his full attention. "I absolutely adore this house and how perfect it is. I mean, you honestly have no idea." He doesn't. I'm astonished and awestruck at how we both seemingly ended up living in two extremely similar homes during our time apart. "But, your walls are cold and bare. I know that's not really any of my business, but I was kind of excited to see how you expressed yourself creatively inside here." I shrug.

He steps close to me, wrapping his arms around my lower waist where they come to rest just above my ass. "Fancy pants, it's very much your business. You see, I was wishing and waiting for the other part of me…I guess you could call her my creative half, to come back. Because she does bring out the best in me, and quite literally fills a void."

My heart flip flops and my heart feels like it's about to burst out of my chest as it leaps for his. I feel his hands slide lower until they stop on my ass cheeks. My God he's being so gentle, and his touch is so soft, goosebumps erupt all over my body.

I reach up and run my hands through his hair before I lower my gaze back and into his eyes. Staring back at me is nothing but pure love and gratitude, hinted with an animalistic desire that burns through my existence.

He lifts me up and naturally my legs hug his waist as he continues to stare at me as he walks us into his bedroom. Once we're in there, he lays me down onto my back. My center feels like it's melting from the intense fire burning inside me. I need to feel him in every way possible and I watch as he quickly strips himself free from all of his clothing. My eyes shoot straight down to his large cock that indicates we both have the same need.

He smirks menacingly at me and I want to scream for him to take me now. He pulls me forward, removing my pumps first before he wastes no time removing the rest of my clothing. I fall backward and scoot myself more toward the headboard while he climbs over and on top of me, never allowing me to get too far away. Hovering over me, he lowers his face and I feel his tongue make contact with my flesh as he slowly drags his tongue from my clit, all the way to my collarbone. He's awakened and aroused every nerve in my body and I ache to feel him be inside of me. "Blaine," I call out breathlessly.

"I'll get there, Tara," he replies in a gravelly, animalistic tone which only increases my desire and primal need to be one again with him. He cups my breasts and sucks on each one, never giving one anymore attention than the other. He takes one of my nipples between his teeth and gently tugs until a moan escapes me. He begins the same assault on my other breast as I feel his hand go between our bodies and travel down to my opening. Momentarily he circles and rubs my clit sending sparks and bolts of electricity throughout my body and in response, I arch my back. I feel him insert two fingers inside me and he hooks them as he did before, managing to find that certain spot that sends me soaring. "Let it go, Tara," he says in a deep, raspy, commanding tone. "Make way for me, baby." And with that I surrender and release. "Ahh, good girl," he praises me as I'm still riding out the ecstasy wave he's gifted me.

He pulls his fingers from me and I can see the glistening remnants of my orgasm on them. He pulls his eyes from mine and focuses on his fingers, eyeing them like a prize before he licks them. Methodically, he traces his tongue upward on each digit, leaving me shocked. "Mmm," he mumbles through now closed eyes before they shoot back open and find mine. "I have waited so long to taste you again."

He takes a hold of his stiff cock and lines it up with my slick opening while rubbing it up and down my slick folds. I feel another orgasm swirling inside my belly watching him play with me using himself. He steadies himself and I brace myself for impact as he slowly sinks into me, filling me entirely. I can no longer contain the moans and pants that haven't asked permission to leave my throat. I hook my arms under his, until my nails make contact with his back as I pull him closer to me. Continuously he drives his cock inside of me hard, only to pull himself back out slowly. I retaliate by bucking my hips upward toward his pelvis as I claw my nails down his back. He looks at me and grins, knowing he's winding me up inside so tight that I am on the brink of an enormous eruption. He picks up his pace and we begin to meet each other thrust for thrust as I feel my walls begin to clench. "Play with yourself, Tara. I wanna watch you help bring us to climax together." I lower my fingers until I make contact with my clit and begin to circle and rub it while I watch his cock glide in and out of me effortlessly.

"Oh, God!" I shout, as I feel the intense orgasm stir with fury inside of me.

"Not God, Tara. What's my name?" he growls.

"Blaine," I whisper through clenched teeth.

"I can't hear you," he replies, still pumping himself in and out of me without mercy.

"Blaine! Yes! Blaine!" I scream as I feel my orgasm release as it drips down my ass cheeks, probably pooling on the sheet.

After a few more intense pumps, he stills himself as he roars, "Ahhhh! Yes, Tara!"

Sweaty and tired, he falls down beside me on the bed and I ache internally at the loss of him being inside of me.

BLAINE

I COULD LAY HERE AND WATCH THE RISE AND FALL OF HER chest as she sleeps so peacefully for the rest of my life. How can one person be so beautiful even while they're in a deep slumber? After our reconnecting encounter last night we showered, and I made her mine twice more. After the shower, we laid in front of my fireplace and caught up on our lost time before our bodies danced together harmoniously alongside the flames.

I wanna do something special and nice for her, but I really suck at the whole romantic thing. Especially when I'm too entranced at her beauty. I hesitantly pull my eyes from her and eventually decide on making her breakfast in bed. Now, I'm no cook like Ma is, but I'm sure I could whip something up.

I pull my boxer briefs up and put a t-shirt on before heading into the kitchen. Once I'm in there, I get lost looking in my bare pantry. Ah, I've got pancake mix, but quickly realize I have no eggs. After observing the situation I'm reduced to toast with butter and strawberry jam with a side of orange juice. Nothing about that seems filling or romantic and I refuse to leave her to go to grocery shopping. Fuck it, toast and juice is better than nothing.

The gentle knock at my door nearly went unnoticed thank fuck, because Tara is still sleeping. She must be exhausted after everything last night, so whoever's here better come bearing a balanced breakfast while ready to catch my wrath should they wake her.

Looking out the peephole, I notice it's my ma alongside the other three stooges. Emmit, Sharla and Jett. I scrub my face with my hand before I open it with my finger covering my lips, ordering them to be quiet. "Stop right there." I stand in the frame of my door, blocking it as Sharla peeks around me.

"We know she's in here, Blaine. We saw her car parked at the bar. Gah, I knew y'all would be back together. It was too fated to happen any other way," Sharla whispers, holding Jett on her hip.

"And you can see her after we've had some more quality time together. It's not up for debate as I'm sure she is eager to see all of you as well. Now, go back home. In fact, knowing Tara, she'll want to come by and see you all later today. Right now? I'm being stingy. Don't take this personal, but leave," I tell them in a stern whisper with gritted teeth.

"Here, you scrooge. I made some breakfast sandwiches. Two for each of you because I wasn't sure just how famished the two of you might be after…well…you know?" my ma says, suggesting she knows that we've had sex and probably more than once.

I cover my face in near-embarrassment. "Stop. Stop right there, Ma." I lean in and kiss her cheek while taking the bag from her. "You're definitely saving my ass right now as I have nothing that really goes together for, well, any meal."

"I know, son. Hence the sandwiches. Okay. We'll get out of your hair, honey." She pats my arm before turning her back to usher my brother and Sharla away too.

Once I know they're gone, I place the sandwich on a plate

and pour a glass of orange juice. Placing them both on a plate, momentarily I stare at it. It's missing something, but I don't know what. Hell, maybe I'm just being overly nervous because I know she'd have loved it even it had been just toast. I glance out the backdoor and notice the colorful flowers I had planted, so I decide to go pick just one. After strategically garnishing the rest of the tray with the flower, I make my way into my bedroom and notice Tara is already awake holding the sheet up against her bare breasts. She's sitting up and I watch as she yawns before smiling in my direction.

"Morning, fancy pants. Did you sleep well?" I sit down beside her, placing the tray between us.

"Mhmm," she murmurs before rubbing her eyes.

"Good. I wanted to let you sleep in as long as I could, but I knew you also needed to eat something."

She glances down at the tray between us and her eyes grow wide as she tries to focus more intently. She picks up the flower and casts her soul-catching eyes at me. "It's a Dahlia."

I nod. "Yes. I have a landscaper that comes by twice a month to care for my yard. I knew I wanted some flowers, and when I saw these, they made me think of you. So, these are what I had him plant. Do you not like them?"

Her eyes light up and beam like the sun as a smile crosses her beautiful lips. "They're my favorite actually. She stands, wrapping the sheet around her body and makes her way to the far window in my bedroom with the flower still in her hand. I follow behind her as she opens the drapes and blinds. "Wow," she replies at the sight of my colorful blanket of Dahlias.

Wrapping my arms around her waist from behind, I rest my chin on the top of her head. "I'm glad you like them and I'm even more glad they're your favorite."

She stands, staring into my backyard for what feels like an eternity and I know she's deep in thought, but about what, I'm unsure. "What are you thinking about, fancy pants?"

"Just how good it feels to be home," she turns her face and purrs against my beating heart.

The end…for now

EPILOGUE

TARA
Six Months Later

RAY AND GWEN WERE BOTH GIVEN THE MAXIMUM sentence which surprised us all considering Gwen had no priors. I didn't attend the hearing as I felt I'd already closed that chapter in my life. I've officially moved in with Blaine and so has Carmen. I've officially found my calling as a waitress, although most days Blaine would disagree, but I enjoy serving others and feeling like I've earned my way.

Emmit and Sharla are engaged and she finally graduated and got her degree about a month ago. She's been applying all over which has Emmit unhappy to say the least. Other than three doctors' offices and one hospital in this town, you have to travel several hours to get to the nearest medical office. She's adamant that she wants to work in the pediatric field. That presents its own challenges considering the nearest pediatric office that she recently applied to is in Oklahoma.

As we close the bar, we begin our routine of nightly cleaning, counting money, and restocking.

I'm wiping down a table when Sharla comes storming out of the back with Emmit hot on her heels. "It's my damn career, Em! I've worked too damn hard for this to decline the offer now! Why don't you take a fucking sabbatical and come with us? It's not like you can't afford to," she hollers as I feel like I'm intruding on something that should be private.

"You know why!" Emmit's voice booms throughout the bar and I jump. "It's not up for discussion."

"Here." Blaine hands me a glass of whiskey and I notice he's made himself one too. "You not used to this by now, fancy pants? All they've done the past month is bicker and argue. It's like watching a verbal tennis match." He chuckles, taking a seat at the table I was wiping.

Sharla continues to lash out and I take a seat next to Blaine as I feel a yawn creep in. "So, you want me to announce this here? Right now? Without your ma around or anything, fine!" She turns to me and Blaine. "I'm pregnant! There. You happy now? Not exactly how I imagined we would tell your family, but hey, two down and one to go!" She cups her face before bursting into tears as she hastily retreats with Emmit following closely behind.

I hear him call to her, "Shar, wait. Fuck."

"Well." Blaine looks at me. "Wasn't expecting that. Although she has been rather moody lately." He holds his glass up and my eyes find his. "Either way, a new addition to the family is always a welcomed one, huh? Aren't you gonna toast with me?" My heart hammers against my chest. "Oh, come on. I know I have a sometimes warped sense of humor, but are you really too upset or tired to share one drink with your man after a long night and huge declaration?"

I swallow thickly before I slide the liquor back toward him. "Yeah, I know your sense of humor. But I hope you can find such excitement in what I have to tell you." His face suddenly goes serious and he lowers his glass. "I can toast with you, but you're going to need to make me something non-alcoholic, Blaine." His eyes grow wide and I watch as some of the color appears to drain from his face.

"You're fucking scaring me, fancy pants." I watch him

swallow hard as he stares intently at me, as if he's waiting for me to announce the impending apocalypse.

"Blaine, I'm also pregnant," I blurt out, restraining the tears I feel pooling in my eyes. I know this wasn't planned and I fucking pray he doesn't flip shit on me. Nothing. I get absolutely nothing for what feels like an eternity. I swear this man doesn't even blink. "Please say something. Because I'm freaking out over here. I found out this morning and I know this is the last thing we both expected. But I did everything right. I took my pill on time. I-I just don't know…" The clear drops have escaped my eyes and fall down my cheeks and over my lips, leaving their salty taste on my lips.

"You…I mean…And you're certain?" he stammers out.

"I took about four different tests, and all came back positive. I called my doctor and made an appointment. But Carmen says those things are pretty damn accurate," I reply, looking down, picking away at the nail I chipped earlier tonight.

I notice him stand and inch closer to me before he wraps his hands underneath my arms, lifting me up until I wrap my legs around his waist. He tips my chin up to look at him before he wipes the tears from my cheeks. "So, you and I made a baby?" I nod. "I'm gonna be a daddy?" I nod again before he presses his lips to mine. "Are you sad about this?"

"No, honestly. I'm excited, but I have been anxious all day wondering how you would react to such unexpected news," I admit.

That mischievous grin that sets my soul on fire curls upward on his face. "Can you honestly name one thing about you and I that has been planned? Not even the way we met, or the way we came back together can be considered normal or planned. So, why would our baby?"

I smile before I let small giggle escape. "I suppose you're right when I really think about it."

"And I suppose we're gonna be needing a bigger house." He twirls me around before he sets me down.

"I think you're right, Mr. Knight."

This book is dedicated to all of my devoted readers. Thank you for taking a chance with me on this new journey and adventure. If it weren't for your continued faith in me, none of this would be possible. As always, words simply never seem to quite do justice to the magnitude of graciousness I feel for you all. Hopefully, this simple 'thank you' from the depths of my heart will suffice.
Much love always,

~Kayce

ACKNOWLEDGMENTS

Elaine Holcomb PA – Thank you for your never-ending faith in me and my ability to write a book out of my "comfort zone."

Liberty Parker – While writing this book, life threw some challenges my way. You immediately stepped up and came to my rescue. You're not only my sister, but my best friend. Thank you for always being there for me no matter our ups and downs. <3

Erin Osborne – When I pitched this idea that I had stirring around in my head, you encouraged me to go for it. Your unyielding faith and belief in me helps keep me going. I'm proud to call you a true and best friend.

Darlene Tallman – All I can say is remember "hell trip?" Little did any of us know just how much that one trip would challenge and redefine our friendship. It was good before, but now, it's great! Thank you for helping me last minute and never leaving my "side."

Sharon Renee PA – I know I brought in on this wild ride toward the end of this particular book, but you happily stepped up. When you quickly found out that your responsibilities were going to increase, again, you jumped right in. I truly cannot express the gratitude I have for you.

Tara Hettel – This one's all you, girl! I hope you thoroughly enjoyed the story of Tara and Blaine. <3

Kim Richards – Last but never least, you will always and forever be acknowledged in each of my books. You hopped on this 'crazy train' long before it became more than just a simple a hobby. You loved and encouraged me to push forward, and I have. Love you to bits!

ABOUT THE AUTHOR

Kayce lives in Texas where she was born and raised. She has five beautiful children, one grandchild, and four fur babies whom she adores. She's a huge animal lover and would save (and house) every animal if she could. If she's not writing, she's probably listening to music while cooking, cleaning, or doing laundry. The latter of which she would tell you she detests most in life. She loves to read and hang out with friends and family.

OTHER WAYS TO KEEP UP WITH THIS AUTHOR

Newsletter sign up: http://eepurl.com/dILhSb
Email: kaycekyle35@gmail.com
Kayce's Kinky Corner https://www.facebook.com/
groups/1906925202864776/

"One More Knight: Emmit"
The above title will be book two in this duet of the
"Knight Brothers."